Tr

MW01093901

Dune House Cozy Mystery Series

Cindy Bell

Copyright © 2014 Cindy Bell

All rights reserved.

ISBN-13: 978-1503215993

ISBN-10: 1503215997

More Cozy Mysteries by Cindy Bell

Dune House Cozy Mystery Series

Seaside Secrets

Boats and Bad Guys

Treasured History

Hidden Hideaways

Heavenly Highland Inn Cozy Mystery Series

Murdering the Roses

Dead in the Daisies

Killing the Carnations

Drowning the Daffodils

Suffocating the Sunflowers

Books, Bullets and Blooms

A Deadly serious Gardening Contest

Wendy the Wedding Planner Cozy Mystery Series

Matrimony, Money and Murder

Chefs, Ceremonies and Crimes

Bekki the Beautician Cozy Mystery Series

Hairspray and Homicide

A Dyed Blonde and a Dead Body

Mascara and Murder

Pageant and Poison

Conditioner and a Corpse

Mistletoe, Makeup and Murder

Hairpin, Hair Dryer and Homicide

Blush, a Bride and a Body

Shampoo and a Stiff

Cosmetics, a Cruise and a Killer

Lipstick, a Long Iron and Lifeless

Camping, Concealer and Criminals

Table of Contents

Chapter One

The wooden slats on the wraparound porch creaked mournfully as Suzie walked across them. There were still some repairs that needed to be made to the old house which was affectionately known as Dune House. Suzie and her best friend, Mary, had recently renovated the house so it could be run as a bed and breakfast once again. For just a moment Suzie wondered how many people had walked across those same wooden slats. She knew that her aunt, uncle, and their son, Jason, had lived in this house.

Her uncle was almost a total recluse when he died leaving the house to her. His life was shrouded with mystery as she had not known him very well. She had enjoyed getting to know her cousin, Jason, who was much younger than she was and a police officer for the fine, tiny town of Garber. Now the grand old home, a mansion compared to the other houses in town, belonged to Suzie. But what about all of the other lives that had passed through it? Suzie's questions were forgotten when she reached the small table with two chairs. Mary was gazing out over the water, her expression filled with longing. Suzie was fairly certain that she hadn't noticed her approach.

"I made us coffee," Suzie said softly as she sat down across from her friend. Mary's auburn hair was loose and flowing around her shoulders. When the wind teased it, the streaks of gray nestled in the thick strands glistened in the sunlight. She had such a loving spirit in Suzie's opinion that it seemed to be reflected in her soft, kind features and culminated in her warm, brown eyes. Mary rarely had a cross word to say about anyone but she was always willing to listen to Suzie's rants about everyone and everything. The pair seemed to balance each other out as friends.

They were both in their fifties, but couldn't be more different if they tried. Suzie's life had been filled with adventure and even a little danger. She dressed as fashionably as possible and did her best to keep up with technology and politics. Her hair was cut in a short and sassy style and was dyed a brassy gold that she felt took about ten years off her face. She was quick to judge and quicker to put someone in their place if she felt they were out of line. But Mary always had a way of calming her down.

Now that they were sharing their lives again on a daily basis there was a sense of completion within Suzie, as if she had been missing Mary all of these years. Meanwhile Mary had been raising her family, confiding her struggles with her husband only with Suzie, and playing the part of the happy wife and mother. Despite the fact that Suzie had been in harrowing situations with some dangerous people, she still believed that Mary was the stronger of the two for not planning her husband's demise long ago. That subtle strength rose to the surface the moment that Mary became aware of Suzie's presence.

"Oh Suzie, thank you," Mary drew a smile to her lips. Suzie could tell that it took some effort to do so.

"Are you all right, hon?" Suzie asked as she set the coffee in front of Mary. Then she sat across from her. She was surprised to see Mary looking down-hearted considering that they had almost finished renovating the house and were ready for opening day tomorrow.

"I'm all right," she replied with a wistful smile. "Just thinking about the past."

"I know that you must be missing home," Suzie offered gingerly. Suzie had never been terribly attached to any one place. She preferred to travel, and often did during her career as an investigative journalist. It wasn't until she had switched paths and become an interior decorator that she had settled in one place for any length of time. Mary on the other hand had married and stayed in the same home while she raised her children. She endured many years of neglect by her husband, and when her children went to college she had finally divorced. It had been a tumultuous time for her, and with Suzie inheriting Dune House the two friends had agreed to start a new life together. It hadn't been a huge change for Suzie, but for Mary it was a total change of pace.

"It's not home I'm missing," Mary replied with a sigh. "I guess you can have empty nest syndrome wherever you are. I know the kids are fine, they are adults now with their own lives. But, I still miss them."

Suzie had to bite her tongue. She had a secret that she was keeping from Mary, and she didn't want to ruin the surprise. She had never had children of her own, but she had kept in contact with Mary throughout her children's lives, and in many ways she felt a deep connection with them.

"I'm sorry, Mary, I know that must be hard,"

she reached out and gave her friend's hand a gentle squeeze.

"I'm sorry, I don't want to dampen the excitement," Mary said with a shake of her head and smiled brightly. "I'm looking forward to the opening. Is Paul going to be here for it?" she arched an eyebrow mischievously.

Suzie knew that Mary was changing the subject for her sake, and normally she would steer it right back and talk through her friend's feelings. But knowing what she did, she felt relief when the subject shifted.

"He said he will be, but with him going in and out on the boat, he can never be sure," Suzie shrugged a little. She tried not to blush. Paul was a local fisherman who she had met and formed a quick bond with. He had made it clear to her when he tried to kiss her for the first time that he was interested in more than friendship, but Suzie wasn't sure if she was ready to take that next step.

"I'm sure he'll be here," Mary said with confidence. "I wouldn't put it past him to swim if he needed to."

"Ha!" Suzie laughed. "He probably would," she smiled as she thought of Paul. He was a strong man with broad shoulders. His job was physically demanding at times, and it helped him stay fit well into his fifties. Suzie thought his gray eyes were a direct reflection of the open sea just before dawn, which was often when he would set out on his fishing trips. His face was weathered by the wind and the sun, which Suzie found incredibly attractive and interesting, as if it contained memories of his life that his mind might not even recall. She had an image of him swimming towards her across the roughest seas and smiled shyly. Suzie hadn't come to Dune House looking for romance. She thought that was in her past. But Paul seemed to be determined to make it part of her present.

"I can't believe we already have guests booked

for the opening," Mary said with pride in her voice, bringing Suzie's thoughts back to reality. "I have a feeling this place is going to be quite successful."

"With this beauty surrounding it, how could it not be?" Suzie tipped her head towards the water that stretched out endlessly before them. Suzie had a few memories of visiting Dune House when she was very young. It had always seemed like paradise to her. To end up being a part of it, was an amazing thing for her.

The two friends fell into a comfortable silence as the waves rolled in. Suzie sipped her coffee while Mary slowly stirred hers. They had always been close enough to sit together without saying a word. Just as Mary lifted her mug to take a sip of her coffee, Suzie heard a beeping horn from the front of the house. Her eyes widened. She glanced at her watch. She hadn't realized how late it was.

"Who could that be?" Mary asked as she put down her mug of coffee.

"It must be our first guest," Suzie said mischievously as she stood up from the table.

"What?" Mary asked with surprise. "We didn't have any guests that were supposed to arrive yet! I haven't even checked the rooms to make sure they are ready!"

Suzie tried not to laugh at her friend's panic. She felt a little guilty for not revealing the truth. But she had made a promise that she wouldn't.

"The rooms are perfect, Mary," she assured her. "Let's go greet our first guest!" she said happily.

"Oh, all right," Mary frowned. She was clearly not happy about the surprise guest. Suzie knew that would change in an instant. They walked around the porch to the front of Dune House. There was a taxi in the long driveway. A man was standing beside the taxi.

"Oh my!" Mary gasped as she set eyes on the man. "Oh, is it really you, Ben?" she cried out as she ran down the steps towards him. She ignored the aching in her knees as she threw her arms around her son and hugged him tightly. Suzie stood at the top of the steps that led up to the porch, grinning from ear to ear. She and Ben had planned the little surprise, but it had been Ben's idea.

"Oh, I've missed you, Mom!" Ben said and held her close. Not all men in their early twenties would be so affectionate, but Mary had doted on both of her children with such love and affection as they grew up that they were very loving in return. It brought a hint of tears to Suzie's eyes to see her friend so blissfully happy as the two walked up the steps onto the porch.

"Catherine wanted to be here, too, but she had some classes she had to complete," Ben paused and smiled at Suzie before looking back at his mother. "We just want you to know how proud we are that you and Suzie have done this. It's really great to see you so happy, Mom."

"Happy?" she grinned. "I'm over the moon!" she hugged him again. "You have to tell me about everything. How is school going? Have you met any girls?"

Ben rolled his eyes and laughed. "Plenty of time for that, Mom. I'm going to stay for a couple of days after opening day. So, if you need any help with anything, I'm here to offer it!"

Suzie felt a sense of pride as she studied Ben. In many ways he was a reflection of his mother with auburn hair cut short and deep brown eyes, but he had the strong English features that belonged to his father of a slightly hooked nose and slender face. Ben had always been a good, young man, but he had some trouble during his teens. He was vying for his father's attention, which was not easily given. He had grown through that stage, and now he was a bright, young adult who she believed could accomplish anything.

"Suzie, you look fantastic," Ben said as he opened his arms to her. Suzie hugged him warmly. "And so does this place," he added as he ran his eyes over Dune House. The house rose majestically on the top of the sloping hill. Its turreted roof and dramatic windows made it look like something out of an old movie. The wraparound porch gave it a sense of being a home, but its sprawling size made it appear to be a mansion. With the sea as its backdrop there was no way to deny its beauty.

"Yes, we're pretty happy with it," Suzie said with a modest smile. She couldn't imagine a more beautiful place to live. It had been a lot of work, but it was well worth the effort, and she had really enjoyed decorating each of the larger suites to reflect a different style or place.

"Mary, why don't you take him down to the beach?" Suzie suggested. She could tell her friend was still in shock from the surprise.

"Great idea," she said. "Leave your shoes here, Benny, you won't need them," she grinned.

Suzie watched the moment as the two walked out across the sand. They had such a similar gait, Mary's only weighted slightly by the trouble she had with her knees. She smiled fondly to herself as her mind flicked through memories of Ben growing up, then she turned back towards the house. As Suzie stepped back into the house, she heard her cell phone ringing. She hurried over to where she had it charging on the kitchen counter. She was hoping that it would be Paul. She smiled when she saw his name on the caller ID.

"Good morning," she said as she answered the phone.

"Good morning," he replied warmly. "I was wondering if the surprise went smoothly?"

"It did," Suzie replied giddily. "Mary is very happy to see him."

Suzie had shared her plans with Paul. In fact they had been talking every day and seeing each other several times during the week. He had helped with the final touches to Dune House, and put her in contact with local tradesmen when she needed them.

"Well, it might be nice if they have a night to catch up," Paul said in a casual way.

"Yes, I'll probably just hole up in my room tonight and let them have some space," Suzie agreed. She knew that Mary and Ben might want to have that time to talk about some private issues regarding the divorce and Ben's future plans.

"Or you could join me for dinner," Paul suggested slyly.

Suzie's heart skipped. She had been avoiding being alone with Paul. When he was over Mary was always with them. Since he had tried to kiss her and she had turned away offering only her cheek, she had been anxious about what it would be like the next time she was alone with him. It wasn't that she didn't want to kiss him, in fact she had been spending quite an embarrassing amount of time imagining what it would be like. She just wanted to know that she would be ready. Going to dinner together would mean that they would be alone. Could she handle it?

"That would be lovely," Suzie began. "But..."

"Oh boy," Paul sighed with a subtle laugh. "I understand," he said before she could even give him an excuse. Suzie wondered how long he would tolerate her pushing him away. She didn't want to give him the impression that she didn't want to be with him.

"I was going to say, but I want to go to Cheney's," she said swiftly. "I'm dying for some pasta."

"Cheney's it is," Paul said sounding pleased. "Around six?"

"I'll be ready," Suzie promised. When she hung up the phone her mind was buzzing with excitement and uncertainty.

"That sounded promising," Mary said as she

walked into the kitchen.

"You heard me?" Suzie smiled shyly.

"I heard you trying to blow him off, again," Mary pointed out with a grim smile. "But that last part, I liked."

"I know, I know, I just feel so torn," Suzie sighed.

"Trust me, Suzie," Mary said with a distant look in her eyes. "The love of a man who truly cares for you is worth the risk."

Suzie was surprised that Mary would say that after all she had been through. Her friend was always very wise, and knew just what to say in any given situation.

"We're going to dinner, I thought that would give you and Ben some time to catch up," Suzie explained.

"It will be perfect," Mary nodded. "We'll order in and I'll find out the truth about these girls I've been hearing about."

"Girls?" Suzie laughed.

"Uh huh, seems to be more than one," Mary grimaced.

"He's young, Mary, remember that," Suzie chuckled.

"I know, he's getting settled in his room right now. I can't believe you two kept this from me!" Mary said with playful anger.

"I'm sorry. It really was his idea. He wanted to show you his support," Suzie smiled. "You've raised a really amazing young man, Mary."

"How did that happen?" Mary laughed and shook her head.

"I know just how it happened," Suzie smiled proudly. "Now, help me figure out what to wear, hmm?"

"Sure," Mary agreed. As they went through Suzie's closet it felt as if they were right back in high school. It didn't matter how many years had passed, in Suzie's mind she was as young and free as she was the day she had graduated. Giggling over outfits with Mary brought back all of the wonderful times she had spent with her friend. She felt very lucky to be sharing Dune House with her.

"All right, you have three to choose from," Mary said with a final laugh. "I'm going to check over the rooms one last time to make sure everything is in place."

"You've already checked three times," Suzie laughed.

"I know, I know, but one last look won't hurt," Mary grinned as she walked out of the room.

Suzie stood in front of a full length mirror. She looked at the rose-shaded dress that was her first choice for the evening. It was a dusty shade that didn't come close to looking like a little red dress. But she still wondered if she was overdressed. She turned to see the slope of the back, and then sighed. She had already tried on several dresses and this was the one she liked best. With the decision made she changed back into work clothes and went back to work tidying and preparing for the opening.

Chapter Two

By the time Suzie looked up from the work she was doing later that day, it was nearly time to go to dinner. She tossed the dust rags she had been doing a final polish of the railings and fixtures with into a bucket, and walked towards her room. She noticed Ben standing beside one of the tall windows that overlooked the water.

"What are you up to, Ben?" Suzie asked as she paused in the hallway.

"I thought I saw someone," Ben said with a shake of his head. "It looked like they were walking around the house, but when I went out to look no one was there."

"Well, we get a lot of looky-loos," Suzie explained. "Tourists that think it's okay to peek in windows or cut around the property to get to the beach. I wouldn't worry about it too much."

"I guess," Ben said with a slight frown.

"Don't worry, Ben, the place isn't haunted," Suzie teased lightly to try to brighten his mood.

"Are you sure about that?" he asked with an arched eyebrow. "You never know what history this place might hold."

"You have a good point," Suzie said with a smile. "But if there are any spirits hiding out in these walls, they don't seem to be sociable ones."

He laughed at that and nodded. "I guess it could have been a reflection or something. Mom said you're going out tonight?" he leaned back against an end table and studied Suzie for a moment.

"Yes, there's a local fisherman that I've become friends with," Suzie explained as she ran her fingers through her hair. "But I can't go looking like this."

"So, a boyfriend?" Ben asked suspiciously.

Suzie did a double take at his tone. She wasn't used to having her activity monitored by anyone, especially not Ben, who she still saw as the six-year-old boy who would nearly knock the wind out of her every time he hugged her.

"A friend," she clarified sternly.

"Uh huh," he said with little belief in his voice. "What about Mom? Has she been seeing anyone?"

"Benjamin," Suzie said as she crossed her arms. "I think that's something you should ask her about."

"Oh, I know," he said in a more relaxed tone. "I just want her to be happy, Suzie," he said in a soft voice.

Suzie's expression softened as she realized he wasn't trying to spy on his mother, he was hoping that she had met someone.

"You and your sister make her very happy, Ben," Suzie said warmly.

"This is the happiest I've ever seen her," Ben admitted. "Thanks for that, Suzie."

Suzie crossed the distance between them and hugged him. "She'd do the same for me, Ben. Your mother is an amazing woman."

"I know," Ben smiled. "I guess I better get prepared for the interrogation."

"I would highly recommend it," Suzie laughed and walked back towards her room. She took a quick shower and then dried and styled her hair. She added a light amount of make-up and then dressed. It must have taken longer than she thought because when she was done, she heard a knock on the front door of Dune House.

"Paul's here!" Mary called out as she walked past the open door of Suzie's room. Suzie stared a moment longer at her reflection in the mirror, and felt a nervous flutter.

"I'll be right there," she called back as she straightened a few strands of her hair. She turned away from the mirror and snatched up her purse. As she stepped out into the hallway she glanced over the state of the paintings and rug that lined it. Everything looked like it was in place. There was so much to think about before opening. She was glad to have this pleasant distraction.

When Suzie reached the lobby of the house she found Paul waiting for her. He looked quite handsome in a casual suit and she was immediately glad that she had decided to wear the dress. His lips parted with a soft gasp as he took in the sight of her.

"You look stunning," he said softly as he lifted his eyes to hers.

"Can't say that you don't clean up nice," she replied with a light wink. He grinned at her words and offered her his arm. "Oh, wait just a moment, I want you to meet Ben," Suzie said.

"Ben!" Mary called out from the kitchen. "Suzie has someone that she'd like you to meet!"

Ben bounded down the stairs from the second floor. The sight of him brought back memories of when he was just a little boy running down the stairs. Suzie couldn't help but laugh.

"This must be Paul," Ben said with a slow, sly smile as he looked Paul up and down. Suzie's eyes widened. She wondered if he would question him about whether he was a friend or a boyfriend. Ben could be mischievous.

"I am Paul," Paul replied with a broad smile. "You must be Ben," he glanced from Ben to Mary and back again. "You look just like your beautiful mother!"

"Oh Paul," Mary smiled and waved her hand dismissively.

Ben folded his arms across his chest and narrowed his eyes. Suzie was a little surprised by his demeanor.

"And just what are your intentions with Suzie?" he asked in a playfully deepened voice. "She's pretty much my aunt you know."

Paul chuckled at Ben's words. "My intentions

are to fill her up with some delicious pasta and whisk her away for a walk on the beach."

"Well, if you feed me too much pasta you might have to roll me along the beach," Suzie laughed and patted her stomach. "Speaking of which, we should get going."

"Have a good time," Mary said as she waved to Suzie.

"But not too good," Ben warned and raised an eyebrow at Paul.

"Of course," Paul shook his head and laughed. "Funny kid," he said as he led Suzie out onto the porch.

"He's really turned out to be a lovely person," Suzie admitted. "It's pretty wonderful to see."

"You know what else is wonderful to see?" Paul asked as he helped her down the steps and across the driveway towards his car.

"What?" Suzie asked curiously.

"You in that dress," he breathed with a hint of a growl beneath his voice. Suzie giggled.

"I'm glad you like it," she murmured. He opened the car door for her and she settled inside. As she watched him walk around the front of the car she realized just how good it felt to have a man appreciate her the way he did. She enjoyed every aspect of her time with Paul. Now she just had to learn to relax.

"Are you excited about opening day?" Paul asked. He started the car and they began pulling out of the driveway.

"Very excited," Suzie admitted. "We have four guests booked!"

"Wow, that's fantastic," Paul said. He seemed genuinely impressed. "I knew you two could pull it off."

"Not without your help," Suzie said and laid her hand lightly over his. He glanced up at her with a sparkle in his eye and held her gaze for a moment before looking back at the road.

"It was my pleasure," he replied softly. "Seeing you in overalls is almost as lovely as seeing you in that dress."

"I doubt that," Suzie grinned and they both laughed.

***

When Suzie and Paul reached Cheney's it was bustling with customers. Suzie was looking forward to a big plate of spaghetti. She had never been dainty or shy about eating. She had a naturally slim figure but as she was getting a little older she did notice that she was having to work a little harder to maintain it. She didn't care. She was still eating a big plate of spaghetti. And lots of garlic bread. When Paul put his hand on the small of her back to guide her inside, she suddenly wondered if that was a good idea. What if he tried to kiss her again? What if she wanted to kiss him? Garlic breath could ruin a moment.

As they settled at a table in the busy restaurant she sneaked a glance up at Paul. He was reading over the menu. She watched his lips as they pursed together in thought. Her mind drifted to what it would be like to kiss him.

"Suzie, did you find something you'd like?" he asked curiously. Yes, Suzie thought to herself, yes, I think I did. Then she realized he was talking about pasta.

"Oh uh, I think maybe I'll just have some salad," she stumbled out.

"Salad?" he raised his eyebrows. "I thought you wanted pasta?"

"I did," she looked down at the menu. "But now I think maybe something lighter."

Paul closed his menu and put it down on the table. He frowned with concern as he looked at her.

"Are you not feeling well? We can always do this another night," he offered.

"I'm fine, I promise," Suzie said cheerfully.

"Salad," he muttered under his breath and eyed her suspiciously.

"All right, all right, maybe just a little pasta," Suzie laughed.

"That's more like it," he grinned.

Two plates of pasta later, Suzie had plenty of garlic on her breath. She groaned as she sat back in her chair.

"I'm so full!"

"Don't worry, we're going to walk it off," Paul grinned.

Walk it off. That meant that she was going to be alone with him on the beach, with garlic breath. But she didn't care anymore. She couldn't wait to hold his hand and feel the sand under her feet. They shared a piece of pie, too. They were so consumed by the delicious taste that they didn't say much of anything to each other. When the waitress came to take away the plates, Suzie felt her heart beat faster. This meant that soon they would be walking out onto the beach. She was both excited and nervous about being truly alone with Paul. Paul paid the check and then offered his arm.

"Shall we?" he suggested.

"Absolutely," Suzie said as she stood up from her chair and wound her arm through his. "Thanks for dinner."

"Thanks for the company," he replied warmly. As they walked past the host stand in the front of the restaurant, Suzie managed to snag a breath mint from a small dish. She popped it into her mouth when Paul wasn't looking. As they stepped out of the restaurant the sun was offering its last shreds of light. The air was warm but disrupted by a cool breeze from the water.

"Seems like the perfect night for a walk on the beach," Paul said quietly. "Are you up for it?"

"Yes," Suzie replied, trying her best to sound confident and not nervous. She had interviewed powerful people, she had crawled into dilapidated houses, and confronted angry protestors. But being alone with Paul made her feel like a leaf clinging to a tiny branch in the middle of a hurricane. As they drove back towards Dune House Paul brought up the opening.

"What guests do you have booked?" he asked.

"We have four booked right now. One single man, one single woman, and a married couple," Suzie replied.

"Two singles, eh?" Paul smiled. "Maybe you'll have a love connection."

"Maybe," Suzie replied. He pulled into the long driveway of Dune House. Suzie could see lights on in the living room, so she knew someone was still up. As she stepped out of the car Paul slid his hands into hers. It felt so natural to have the warmth of his skin against the curve of her palm. They walked down a few wooden steps to the beach, which was almost empty. It was a week night, and though the beach was gorgeous, locals were used to having it any time they wanted so they didn't populate it too much during the evenings. Stars were beginning to stretch across the sky. Suzie left her shoes by the steps. Paul followed suit, along with his socks. They strolled in silence right at the water's edge, taking in the beauty of the night.

"Suzie," Paul said, breaking the silence with the flow of his slightly rough voice. "Can we stop for a moment?" he asked and tightened his grasp on her hand. Suzie's heart jumped. She felt a buzz creeping through her body that made her nerves feel as if they were sparking.

"Sure," she paused and stepped a little further into the water so that she could feel its ebb and flow.

"I know that you have so much going on right now," he said gently. "I really appreciate you taking time out for dinner."

"I couldn't think of a better way to spend my evening," she said in a murmur and glanced up at him shyly. The moment her eyes met his, Paul reached for her. She felt the spray of the water against her ankles as he tangled his fingers in her hair. Her eyes fell shut and her chin tilted upward. The warmth of his lips drew close to hers. This was it. This was the moment. When the silk of his lips embraced her own, she felt as if her entire body was being swept away by the tug of the waves. She had scoffed at love before, at the pop of a leg, or the swoon of a woman being kissed. But in that moment she believed in it all. It was all proving to be true. His fingers rubbed gently along the rise of her neck as the kiss continued. When it finally broke, she stared into his eyes. He seemed fairly breathless himself, his hands still gently encircling the back of her neck.

"Wasn't too bad was it?" he asked, a hint of insecurity in his eyes. "I'm a little out of practice," he admitted.

"Wasn't bad at all," Suzie replied in a whisper. "But maybe we could both use a little more practice," she murmured as she pushed her lips back against his. He smiled through the kiss and they both naturally fell into the rhythm of passion. When the kiss broke again, Paul wrapped his arms around her. The sound of the waves crashing surrounded them both. Suzie could hear Paul's heart beating quickly in his chest. She closed her eyes and savored the sound. She had done it. She had officially crossed the line from being friends, to being something much much more. She still had no idea what that meant, but she didn't regret it.

***

Paul walked her back to Dune House. Suzie waved to him from the porch as she let herself in. She walked through the lobby area into the living room. Ben and Mary were sitting on the couch each with a drink in hand, talking with laughter in their voices. From the bits and pieces that Suzie heard she assumed they were talking about Ben and Catherine's childhood antics.

"Hello you two," Suzie said.

"Hello to you," Mary said as she glanced from Suzie to the clock on the wall and back to her again. "I wasn't sure what time you'd be home."

"It's a little late," Ben wagged his finger playfully.

"Hmm, I think it's not late enough," Mary grinned.

"On that note, I'm going to head up to bed," Ben said with a short laugh. Suzie was doing her best to hide the blush in her cheeks. Once Ben had gone up to bed Mary drew Suzie into the dining room.

"Now, you and I need some alone time," she said with warmth in her voice.

"That sounds good," Suzie said happily.

Mary sat down at the dining room table. She had placed a candle in the center. As she lit it, Suzie sat down in a chair beside her and breathed a long, slow sigh.

"So, how did it go?" Mary asked eagerly.

"How did what go?" Suzie asked innocently.

"Did it happen? Did you two finally kiss?" Mary demanded impatiently.

Suzie couldn't hide the smile that crept onto her lips. "Maybe," she said quietly.

"Oh I see, maybe," Mary rolled her eyes. "Well, was this kiss that might have happened a good kiss?"

"It might have been the best kiss of my life," Suzie confessed.

"Wow! That's saying a lot!" Mary said with surprise.

"Hey!" Suzie countered. "What are you implying?"

They both broke down into laughter. By the time they had settled again, the candle was burning strong.

"It's amazing to think that we are going to be open for business tomorrow," Mary said as she glanced over the large dining room. It had been redecorated with new paint, new paintings, and new light fixtures. But it was still Dune House, and still had a classic feeling to it.

"It's amazing to me that my life has changed so much in such a short time," Mary said as she set the lighter down. "I didn't think any of this would happen, and now that it has, I can't imagine my life any other way."

"Do you mean that?" Suzie asked. "You don't have any desire to go back?"

"Not an ounce," Mary shook her head. "Ben and Catherine have their own lives. The best part is, whenever they want to visit they will have a place to sleep, and paradise outside to enjoy. I feel alive in many ways for the first time, Suzie, and I have you to thank for that."

"You have yourself to thank for that," Suzie corrected.

"No, I mean it," Mary insisted. "I never would have done anything like this on my own. Because you were so kind and included me in all of this I now have a future I can look forward to. I just can't thank you enough for that."

"I couldn't even count on my fingers and toes the things I have to be thankful to you about, Mary. I'm so glad we got to do this together," she smiled.

"Well, I lit this candle because I figured as we embark on a new journey, we can make a wish. Maybe it's not a birthday wish, but it is still a wish."

The two leaned close to the flame. They closed their eyes. Then they blew out the flame together.

Chapter Three

On the morning of opening weekend, Suzie woke up with a start. She felt as if she had forgotten to do everything. That she wasn't ready for Dune House to open for business. But she didn't have too much time to think about it, because Mary came bursting through her door.

"Are you ready?" she asked happily as Suzie jumped out of bed.

"I am, I just don't know if Dune House is," Suzie said with concern.

"Nope, none of that, we did everything that needed to be done. Everything is ready to go. There's no reason to believe that things will not be ready as they should be today. No worrying!" Mary insisted and clapped her hands together sharply. "Today will be magic!"

"All right, all right, who can argue with an attitude like that?" Suzie grinned and stumbled towards her closet for clothing. After Mary left the room, Suzie dressed. She tried to focus on the opening, but the memory of the kiss she had shared with Paul was pulling at her mind as well. She knew that she would be seeing him later that day as he had promised that he would be there to check on the opening before he left for a couple of nights fishing. She wondered what it would be like to see him in the light of day. She had to admit, the memory was a very nice one. When she joined Mary in the kitchen she already had coffee and a bowl of fresh fruit out to enjoy.

"You are way too good at this," Suzie accused with a smile as she snatched up an apple and crunched into it.

"This, I have been doing all my life," Mary said with a laugh. "I could make breakfast and a pot of coffee in my sleep."

"Good to know," Suzie grinned. After they shared a cup of coffee and some breakfast they both cleaned up the kitchen to ensure that it was spotless. It was not an area for the guests but it was still good to make sure it was in tip-top shape. The lunch foods were already prepped for their early guests. Now, it was just a matter of waiting for the first to arrive. They didn't have to wait long before they heard a car pulling up the front driveway.

"Here we go!" Mary squealed happily. "Our very first guest!"

"Other than Ben of course," Suzie grinned. They walked towards the front door. Outside a car had just parked. It was dusty and old. Nothing fancy. But the man who stepped out of the car was a bit surprising. Suzie noticed right away that he was dressed in an old fashioned way. He had a three piece tan suit with a scruff of a tie at his neck. His glasses were thin rimmed and set low on his nose. His blonde hair was wavy and a little mussed. He was on the shorter side with a slightly round belly. He looked right past Suzie and Mary and instead squinted up at the old house.

"Exquisite," he muttered as he began walking towards the porch. He grabbed the railing and shook it slightly. "Well, this isn't original," he frowned and fixed a glare on Suzie and Mary.

"The original was a safety hazard," Suzie volunteered. "You must be Martin Cote. Welcome to Dune House."

"I am, I am," he said. He seemed very distracted as his gaze passed over the roof before returning to them.

"Let me get your bags," Suzie offered as she stepped down from the porch.

"No, don't do that," he said sharply and hurried past her. He opened the trunk of the car and began sorting through the contents. Suzie and Mary exchanged an anxious look. Suzie frowned. Martin was their first official guest and it didn't seem as if they were getting off to a good start. Martin began lifting equipment out of the trunk. It looked like expensive stuff.

"If you could just show me to my room," he grunted. He insisted on carrying all of the equipment himself. Mary watched him nervously as he maneuvered the steps and made it to the porch.

"Of course, it's just down the hall," she said as she opened the door to the house for him. He had specifically requested a room on the ground floor. Suzie closed the trunk gently. She was a little surprised to see what he was bringing with him, but she knew that dealing with unusual guests was going to be one of the trials of running a B & B. At least he had only booked the room for two nights. She followed Mary back into the house. Mary passed a grimace over her shoulder at Suzie and Suzie raised her eyebrows in response. They had always been able to communicate without having to use words.

"Everything is here for you," Mary explained as she showed Martin the room. He was busy carefully setting his equipment down on the bed.

Suzie spotted a small overnight bag, everything else was cameras, strange electronic readers of some sort, and something that looked like a handheld metal detector.

"There is a small bathroom in this room," Mary opened the door so that he could see. "But if you would prefer, your key also opens the shared bathroom which has a large shower and bathtub that you can use."

"This will be fine," Martin said dismissively. "I'm a bit tired from traveling. So, if you wouldn't mind?"

Suzie nodded. "Of course. We can take care of your registration at dinner tonight. If you'd like I can bring your lunch to the room."

"No, it's fine, I just ate," he said and walked towards them in an effort to essentially push them out the door. Once Mary and Suzie were in the hall he closed the door firmly. Suzie heard the lock engage.

"Wow," she mouthed to Mary who was standing dumbfounded in the hall. She had practiced a long speech to give to every new guest and he had only heard the beginning of it.

Suzie and Mary walked down the hall and back to the kitchen. Once they were sure no one was in earshot, they spoke in hushed voices.

"Don't you think he's a little odd?" Mary asked.

"A little?" Suzie giggled. "I'm sure he'll be friendlier after he has a rest."

"Maybe so," Mary nodded. "I guess we will have to become accustomed to different personalities."

"Morning," Ben said sleepily as he walked down the stairs. He was dressed for the day, but looked like he should have been back in bed.

"Are you feeling okay?" Mary asked with concern. She reached up to feel his forehead.

"I'm fine, Mom," he smiled ruefully and

pushed her hand gently away. "I just stayed up a little too late."

"Talking to all those girlfriends," Mary chastised.

"I don't have a girlfriend, Mom," Ben laughed. "I have girls that are friends."

"Hmm, if you take them out to dinner, they're more than friends," Mary argued. "Aren't I right, Suzie?" she asked. Suzie raised her hands into the air and laughed.

"I'm not getting into the middle of this one!"

"Chicken," Mary accused in a friendly tone.

"Anything you two need help with?" Ben offered.

"Actually, if you wouldn't mind taking a walk around the grounds to make sure that everything looks nice that would be very helpful," Suzie said.

"I can do that," Ben announced. He kissed his mother's cheek and then walked out through the side sliding door that led onto the wraparound porch.

"They are girlfriends," Mary insisted in a whisper.

"Times are different now, Mary," Suzie pointed out. "They call it playing the field I think."

"Hmph," Mary narrowed her eyes. "Sounds like the good life to me. Who is ever going to want to commit if they can play the field instead?"

Suzie raised an eyebrow. It was a good point. "I'm sure Ben will find someone he wants to be more exclusive with eventually," Suzie suggested.

"Not too soon," Mary added.

"Definitely not too soon," Suzie grinned. As she opened her mouth to say something else, they heard a squealing of brakes in the parking lot.

"Must be our next guest," Mary said and smiled grimly. "This should be interesting."

"Hopefully not as interesting as Martin,"

Suzie pointed out in a whisper.

Suzie was walking towards the door when it was suddenly flung open. The woman on the other side paused in the doorway. Her face was almost completely hidden by huge, dark sunglasses. They seemed to be a fashionable pair, and the B & B was by the sea, but it made it nearly impossible to make eye contact.

"Hello, and welcome to Dune House," Suzie said warmly.

"Thank you," the woman replied coolly. She had a thin scarf tied around her dark, straight hair. She looked to be in her thirties, though the dark glasses made it hard to tell for sure. "At least it was easy to find," she said as she scrunched up her nose a little. "This is quite a quaint little town."

The way she said quaint made it definitely not a compliment. Mary stepped up behind Suzie as the woman stepped inside.

"Garber is small, but it has a lot to offer," Mary said happily.

"I hope that's the case," the woman said. "My name is Alice Montreal, I have a reservation."

"Yes of course, Ms. Montreal," Suzie said. "Please allow me to take your bag. Your room is all ready for you."

"Hmm," she nodded a little and then lowered her sunglasses. "So, there is no pool?"

"Well, we thought that might be a little redundant," Mary laughed as she gestured to the large windows that looked out over the wide, open sea.

"I suppose," she shrugged a little and handed over a white, leather overnight bag. When Suzie took it she was surprised by the weight of it. It was such a small bag, it must have had plenty packed into it to make it heavy. Mary chatted to her about special spots in Garber to visit, and meal times at the B & B. Suzie didn't know if the woman was listening as she had pushed her sunglasses back up along her nose.

When they stepped into Alice's room, the woman laughed. "Very funny," she said. She looked over the perfectly made bed, the assortment of books and magazines beside the bed, and the robe hanging on the closet door.

"I'm sorry?" Suzie asked. "What's funny?"

"This can't be my room," Alice said as she turned towards Suzie. "It's so tiny."

"Cozy," Mary piped up.

"Tiny," Alice argued. "Is there even a bathroom in here?" she asked.

"Right here," Suzie said smoothly. She was doing her best to hide the annoyance in her voice. She opened the door to the small bathroom.

"But there's only a tiny shower," Alice complained. "This is nothing like the room that I saw on the website."

"Well, we do have an assortment of rooms," Mary said hesitantly.

"But you made a reservation for the single studio room," Suzie pointed out. "That's what this is. There's room enough for a table and chairs, an easy chair, the bed. Plus you have a view of the water," Suzie explained.

"The room I saw was huge," Alice insisted, she was irritated.

"But that is not the room you paid for," Suzie explained in a soft tone.

"That's false advertising!" Alice huffed. "I can't believe this. I knew I shouldn't have taken a chance on a rinky dink place like this…"

"Now, wait just a moment," Mary said quickly when she saw anger rising in Suzie's expression. "It's our opening weekend, and we're not booked solid. I understand there's been some confusion. Perhaps we could upgrade you to one of the larger rooms?"

Suzie did her best not to wince. She could already see that Mary was going to be much better at customer service than she was. But the woman was rubbing her up the wrong way. The last thing she wanted was to give her the larger room.

"I'm not paying a penny more," Alice said firmly. "This is supposed to be a weekend getaway and I'm already feeling very stressed."

Mary met Suzie's eyes questioningly. Suzie could tell that Mary wanted to agree to upgrade the room without charging more. She trusted Mary's judgment.

"Fine, we can arrange something," Suzie said calmly. "I'll review the website and make sure that the pricing and room selection is clearer," she added, though she knew it was perfectly clear. "Perhaps you'd like to wait on the porch with a nice glass of home brewed tea while we get the room prepared for you?"

"Just water will be fine," Alice said with a

sniff. She plucked her bag from the bed where Suzie had placed it. Then she turned and strutted out of the room.

"I'm sorry, Suzie, I hope you don't think that I was too interfering," Mary said quickly.

"You handled it much better than I ever could have," Suzie replied with a shake of her head. "I don't know how you can keep your cool."

"I've been a referee for a long time," she laughed softly. "Which room should I move her to?"

"Put her in the Venice suite," Suzie suggested. "Maybe that will appease her."

The Venice suite was decorated to remind guests of the city of Venice, Italy. It had luxurious tapestries as well as paintings of the city and even a functioning water feature.

"Are you sure?" Mary asked with surprise. "That's one of our most expensive rooms, it even has the garden tub in the bathroom."

"It's opening weekend," Suzie replied. "I think we can afford to spoil the guests a little. Besides, the last thing we want is bad word of mouth."

"Okay," Mary nodded and headed off to prepare the room. As Suzie walked back towards the kitchen she heard the front door open and close. She wasn't expecting the next guest for another hour, but she knew schedules could run early or late. With a smile she walked into the lobby area. Paul was waiting to greet her with a bouquet of fresh, local flowers.

"Happy opening day," he smiled over the top of the flowers.

"Thank you," Suzie beamed. She looked away from him shyly as she took the flowers. They were a lovely gesture, and Suzie gave them a light sniff. "They're beautiful."

"How is it going so far?" he asked curiously as he followed her into the kitchen. She found a vase and placed the flowers in some water.

"It's going," Suzie replied with a wry smile. "Let's just say, I'm glad Mary is good with customer service."

"And you're not?" he asked teasingly. "I would never believe that!"

"I try," she said with a dramatic sigh.

"Well, don't worry, you'll get used to it soon enough," Paul said. "If not, I can always take you out for an escape on the boat."

"I'll hold you to that," Suzie smiled as she rested her elbows on the kitchen counter. Paul leaned close. Her breath caught in her throat as she realized he was going in for a kiss. She returned a light peck.

"Wow-wee is he included in the room rate?" Alice asked as she wandered into the kitchen. There was a sign that clearly stated staff only, but she ignored it.

"Sorry ma'am," Paul said with a friendly smile. "I'm taken."

"Shame, you were about the only luxury I've spotted in this place so far," Alice sighed.

Paul glanced at Suzie and tried not to grin. Suzie was doing her best to hide the fact that she was fuming.

"Can I get you anything? A bottle of water? Some tea?" she offered, trying to think of what Mary would do.

"A room would be nice," Alice said haughtily. Suzie could tell that Alice was going to be one difficult guest. Maybe it was best that she got used to it, as Suzie was sure this would be the first of many hard to please guests.

"I'm sure it's just about ready," Suzie offered and felt Paul's hand curve over hers with a calming touch.

"Your room is ready, Alice," Mary said from the doorway of the kitchen.

"It's about time," Alice muttered. Mary rolled her eyes behind Alice's back as she walked down the hall. Once they were gone Suzie turned back to Paul.

"So, am I a liar?" he asked as he looked into her eyes.

"Huh?" Suzie asked as she stared back with some confusion.

"Did I lie, when I said I was taken?" he asked and still held her gaze. Suzie was startled by the question. She had just become comfortable with the idea of kissing him and now he was asking if they were exclusive. She had no idea how to answer that. She thought of Ben playing the field and wondered if that might be what she wanted. Committing to one man was a huge step.

"Well, I..."

"Suzie," Jason said from the entrance of the kitchen. "Sorry if I'm interrupting."

Suzie hid a sigh of relief. "Jason, good to see you," she said. Paul managed not to glare at him.

"Hello Jason, how are things?" he asked in a

mild tone.

"Pretty good," Jason said warmly. "Just wanted to check on the opening."

"It's going well, we already had two guests check in," Suzie said proudly.

"Good," Jason nodded as he swept his gaze over the kitchen. "Hard to believe this place is going to be so full of life again."

Jason had grown up in Dune House, though his relationship with his father had not been great. That was one of the reasons his father had left the house to Suzie instead of to his son. But the bulk of his wealth, of which the amount was a well-kept secret but was rumored to be quite considerable, was left to Jason.

"Well, you were a big part of making that happen, Jason," Suzie reminded him with a smile. Her cousin was much younger than her, and very handsome in his uniform. He was well liked in Garber and had played a big role in calming some of the locals when they were upset over Dune House being converted back into a B & B. Not everyone was a fan of more tourists in the area. With his thick, red hair and brilliant smile, Suzie could easily see why he was so well received by people. She was just glad that Alice wasn't around to ask if he was a perk.

"I couldn't be happier to see it alive again," Jason admitted. "If you need anything, I'm just a phone call away, all right?"

"Actually, I'd love for you to meet Mary's son, Ben," Suzie said. "He's a little younger than you but he's a good kid."

"I'm not a kid, Suzie," Ben pointed out as he stepped in through the sliding door.

"You're both kids, like puppies," Paul muttered with his usual gruff personality.

"Watch it, Paul," Jason said with a short laugh.

"Jason, this is Ben," Suzie said as Ben walked

towards them. "Ben, this is my cousin, Jason."

"Nice to meet you," Ben said and shook Jason's hand. His eyebrows raised. "Didn't know that Suzie had law enforcement in the family."

"Now you do," Suzie said and grinned. "So, you better behave."

"Who, me?" Ben said with an innocent smile.

"How long are you in town for, Ben?" Jason asked.

"Just a couple more days," Ben replied.

"Well, if you're not busy tomorrow night, I'll take you around town and show you the place. With your mother living here now I'm sure you'll visit more," he added.

"That would be great," Ben smiled eagerly.

"Oh boy, good thing I'm shipping out for a couple of nights, with these two prowling around town," Paul grimaced.

Jason rolled his eyes and Ben smirked.

"I need to get back to my patrol, but, Ben I'll stop by tomorrow after my shift, okay?" he nodded at Ben.

"Sounds good," Ben agreed.

"Everything looked good outside, Suzie," Ben said after Jason left.

"Good," Suzie nodded.

"When do your next guests arrive?" Paul asked.

"Not until this evening, so there's a little time between," Suzie replied.

"That's good, it keeps the chaos to a minimum," Paul chuckled.

"Speaking of chaos, are you ready for your trip tonight? Have you checked the weather patterns?" she asked with some concern. She always worried when Paul was out on the water. He was certainly experienced, but experience didn't mean much against a fierce storm.

"Everything is clear, should be a perfect weekend for your guests to spend on the beach," he pointed out.

"I hope they enjoy it," Suzie said with a hint of pride.

"I'll see you two later," Ben said as he grabbed an apple from the bowl of fruit. "I'm going to catch up on some homework."

Once Suzie and Paul were alone again in the kitchen, the glaring obviousness of his unanswered question seemed to fill the room. He lifted his eyes to hers, and without him speaking a word, she knew that he was still waiting on an answer.

"Oh, I picked up something for your trip," Suzie said as she turned and rummaged in the tall cabinet beside the refrigerator. She heard Paul heave a heavy breath as she avoided the topic again, but he didn't press it. When she turned back with a case of his favorite soda, he grinned.

"Just what I needed," he said happily. "I wasn't sure if I'd have time to get to the store before I left."

"And this," she added and handed him a slim book. "In case you have any time to relax."

He picked up the book and glanced over the title. "Mystery, just what I like," he grinned. "Suzie, if I didn't know any better, I'd say you knew a little bit about me."

"Just a little," she smiled.

He glanced at his watch. "Well, I should be going, I hope that everything else goes smoothly. I'll call you when I get back to land, okay?"

"Okay," she nodded and stood awkwardly before him. He eased the tension by leaning forward for a slow, soft kiss. Suzie felt herself rise up on her toes to lengthen the kiss. When he broke the kiss he winked at her and turned to walk out of the house.

"Maybe when I get back, we can talk?" he

asked as he started to cross through the doorway.

Suzie gulped. "Absolutely," she managed to say. She heard him whistle lightly beneath his breath as he walked through the door.

Suzie felt relieved and disappointed that he was gone. It was so confusing to be so attracted to him, but so unsure of what it was she wanted that attraction to lead to. She was glad there would be a few quiet hours between Alice's arrival, and that of the next guests. Mary returned to the kitchen.

"That woman is high maintenance," she said with a shake of her head.

"Ben taught you that, didn't he?" Suzie grinned.

"Yup," Mary nodded. "Is Paul gone?" she asked.

"Yes, he's shipping out tonight," Suzie explained.

"Too bad," Mary frowned. "Well, at least Alice is settled for the moment. She thought the room was acceptable," Mary laughed at that.

"This is going to take a lot more patience than I thought," Suzie grimaced.

"I'm going to check and see if Martin would like anything," Mary said. As she walked away Suzie sat down in one of the dining room chairs and drew a deep breath to calm herself.

Chapter Four

Everything seemed to have started calming down and Suzie was enjoying a few minutes to herself before the next guests arrived when she jumped at the ear-splitting scream that came from one of the rooms.

"Oh no!" she nearly fell out of her chair as she lunged towards the hallway. "Something terrible must have happened."

"What room is it coming from?" Mary asked as she raced after her. With the second less piercing scream it was clear that it was coming from the Venice suite.

"Alice?" Suzie asked as she knocked on the door, and then opened it. "Alice?" Mary stepped in behind her. Suzie could hear water running in the bathroom. The door was closed, but the light was on.

"Alice, are you in there?" Suzie asked as she

stepped cautiously towards the door. Before she could open it, it flung open. Suzie braced herself expecting a grisly scene, or a wild animal of some sort. Instead it was Alice dressed only in a towel.

"This water is ice cold," she huffed. "I ran a bath, and went to step in, and I probably have frostbite in some terrible places right now!"

"It's cold?" Suzie asked with a frown. "It shouldn't be," she stuck a finger into the water. Although it wasn't ice cold, it certainly wasn't warm enough for a bath.

"I better check the water heater," Suzie said.

"Yes, you do that," Alice said with a disgruntled glare. "Some vacation!"

"Don't worry we'll have it fixed up in no time," Mary assured her.

"I bet," Alice said with obvious annoyance.

Ben must have heard the screaming, too, because he came bounding down the hall. Mary cut him off in the hallway to ensure that he didn't get a view of Alice in a towel.

"What's going on?" he asked with concern.

"For some reason there's no hot water," Suzie said as she stepped out of Alice's room.

"Huh, that's strange," Ben said. "I'll check the water heater."

"Thanks," Suzie said with relief. When he headed downstairs Mary turned to Suzie.

"I'm going to put together a plate of snacks for Alice, maybe that will smooth things over a little," she said and patted Suzie's shoulder. "Don't worry it's just opening weekend hiccups."

"I hope so," Suzie grimaced. She was already adding up in her mind how much it was going to cost to get a new hot water heater. They had depleted their funds quite a bit to get Dune House ready for opening.

A few minutes later Ben returned.

"The water heater looks fine," he said with

some confusion. "But the water level is low. It looks like you must have a leak somewhere."

"A leak?" Mary asked. "But how could the plumber not have seen that when we had the pipes inspected?"

"I don't know, it must have just happened," Ben said with a shrug. "Because I took a shower last night and the water was fine."

"Well, we better get a plumber out here," Suzie said with a grimace. She pulled out her cell phone to call Lester, the plumber they had used before. But his number went to an answering service that stated he was on vacation for the week. "Great, this just keeps getting better and better," she said with a frown.

"Try not to panic," Mary said. "There has to be another plumber in town."

"You know what, I'll call Paul and see if he knows anybody, I'm sure that he's not on the boat yet," she added.

71

"I'll keep Alice happy," Mary said. "I'll try knocking on Martin's door to warn him about the icy shower, too."

"Thanks, Mary," Suzie said as she walked away to make the call. Paul picked up on the first ring.

"Missed me already?" he teased.

"Oh Paul, we've got a problem," Suzie said.

"What's wrong?" he asked, worried by the tone of her voice.

"It looks like there's a leak in the plumbing. The water came out of the pipes but it was ice cold, and now our guests are going to be very unhappy," she sighed. "I tried calling the plumber we used for the inspection, but he's on vacation. Do you know anyone else I could contact?"

"Let me think a moment," Paul said. "Actually, I do. He's from a few towns over but I'm sure he'll come right away. I'll text you the number. Tell him that fisherman Paul sent you."

"Thanks Paul, you're a lifesaver," Suzie sighed.

"Just remember that," Paul said lightly. "Don't let this get you down, sweetheart, everything will be fine."

"That's what everyone keeps saying," Suzie said with some frustration. "Thank you so much," she said. "Have a safe trip."

"I will," he promised her before hanging up the phone. He immediately texted Suzie the phone number. She dialed the number.

"Doug of Doug's plumbing," a boisterous voice said.

"Hi Doug, I'm a friend of fisherman Paul's and he said that you might be able to help me. I have a plumbing crisis, but I'm in Garber," she explained.

"Oh, that's not a problem. I actually don't have any appointments this afternoon so I can come right over. Anything for Paul," he added.

"Thanks so much. It's a big place, are you familiar with Dune House?" she asked.

"Who isn't?" Doug laughed. "Don't worry, I'll be there in thirty minutes."

"Thank you so much," she said before hanging up the phone. She took a deep breath and was starting to feel better.

"I tried knocking on Martin's door, but he's not answering," Mary said as she walked down the hallway. "But I slipped a note under his door for when he wakes up."

"He must have been very tired," Suzie said. "He's been in there for quite some time."

"Are you sure he didn't leave?" Mary asked.

"No his car is in the driveway, and I haven't seen him walk through the lobby," Suzie shrugged.

"Well, some people like to sleep on their vacations," Mary pointed out. "How did the call with Paul go?"

"I've got a plumber coming in thirty minutes," Suzie replied. "Let's just hope it's a quick fix and we can get the pipes running well again."

"I hope so," Mary crossed her fingers. "If not we could always do it the old fashioned way and heat up some water on the stove. We could call it rustic," she laughed.

"That's pretty rustic!" Suzie said, but managed a smile. She couldn't help it. Mary's positive attitude tended to spread.

"Don't worry, Suzie," Ben said. "We'll figure this out."

When the plumber arrived Suzie and Ben were waiting on the front porch for him. She quickly explained the situation and that the water heater seemed to be working properly but without enough water.

"Well, if there are no leaks inside it must be under the house," Doug said. "Let me take a look."

"I'll go with you," Ben offered. He followed

after the plumber. After about twenty minutes the plumber came back to the porch, where Suzie was still waiting, hoping for a good solution.

"Well, you have a damaged pipe under the house," he declared with a frown.

"What? How does that happen?" Suzie asked with concern. "We haven't had any bad weather, and the plumber who did the inspection said that the pipes were fine."

"Honestly, it looks like someone did it on purpose," the plumber said. "The wood around the porch was tugged away so someone could get access."

"How strange," Suzie sighed. "Maybe one of the locals is still unhappy about the B & B. Can you fix it?" she asked with urgency.

"I can," he said with confidence. "I just need to go into town for some supplies. I'll be back soon and should have it fixed in about two hours."

"Oh good," Suzie said. "Thank you, this is our

opening weekend."

"You've got a beautiful place here," he said and headed for his van.

"Hopefully, whoever did this won't try anything else," Ben said with a shake of his head.

"The important thing is that it's getting fixed," Suzie said. "And none too soon, as our next guests are due in an hour. I'd hate to have them drive up in the middle of the repair. But if they do, they do."

Suzie tried to keep herself busy preparing some food for the guests to feast on if they chose. She sent Mary for a walk on the beach with Ben, since there wasn't much they could do until the next guests arrived. She noticed that Martin still hadn't emerged from his room. She decided to walk by the room to see if she could hear any signs of life. As she walked by she noticed that the slip of paper Mary had pushed underneath the door was sticking half out. She thought that was a little strange. If Martin was inside why had he pushed the note out? She lifted her hand to knock on the door, but before she could, Alice came storming down the hall.

"I'm going out for a run on the beach," she said with annoyance. "I expect to be able to shower when I get back."

"Well, hopefully the pipe will be fixed by then," Suzie said as courteously as she could.

"I should hope so," Alice said as she pushed past Suzie. She was dressed in a fancy running suit with her long, black hair in a high ponytail. Suzie shook her head as she watched her go. She was starting to think this guest was more trouble than she was worth, but in some way she could understand her frustration. She glanced at her watch to see that the guests they were waiting for were already an hour late. She hoped they would still show up. She checked the information about them on the small computer they had in the lobby area. They were out of town guests, so it was very possible that they had been delayed. She had forgotten about the note under Martin's door by the time Mary and Ben had returned from their walk.

"We saw Alice on the beach," Mary grimaced. "She's in a real good mood."

"Well, all we can do is try to accommodate her," Suzie shrugged. "Our next guests are almost two hours late."

"Have you heard from the plumber yet?" Ben asked.

"Not yet, I don't think he's back yet. And Alice isn't going to be too happy about that," she sighed.

"With the speed she was running it will probably be a while before she gets back," Mary said.

"That's good at least," Suzie said.

"Oh look, someone's pulling up, looks like the plumber," Ben said. "I'll check to make sure he has all of the parts he needs."

"Thanks," Suzie said. After Ben walked out Mary spotted another car coming up.

"Oh and there's someone else pulling in behind him," Mary said. "Must be the guests we're waiting for."

"We made it!" the woman said breathlessly as she burst through the door. "I didn't think I'd ever get out of that car!"

"Oh Diana, you're being a little dramatic, aren't you?" asked the man who stepped in behind her. He was carrying their bags.

"Maybe if you had asked for directions, it would not have taken us two extra hours to get here, Jim," Diana complained and shook her head. "Men," she rolled her eyes at Suzie and Mary.

"Diana, that's what a GPS is for so you don't have to ask for directions," Jim pointed out as Suzie took a few of the bags from him. "Sorry we're late," he said sheepishly. "Apparently some of the roads leading into Garber aren't accurate on my GPS."

"Small towns can be that way," Suzie said with sympathy. "I'm sorry you've both had such a rough trip. Hopefully we can change that," she smiled.

"All I need is a bathroom and a cup of hot coffee," Diana said.

"Right this way," Mary laughed and led Diana off towards the guest bathroom.

Jim stretched his arms above his head, trying to loosen his back.

"She's right," he admitted. "But I won't tell her that. We drove in circles for about an hour before I finally broke down and asked someone about Dune House. Seems like everyone knows of it!"

"It has been here for a very long time," Suzie explained as she led him to a couch so he could rest. "So, most of the locals even a few towns over know of it."

"It doesn't look old at all," he said with surprise. "I mean, it looks authentic of course. But it's spotless, and looks beautiful."

"Thank you," Suzie said warmly. "Would you like some water? Coffee? Maybe a beer?"

"A beer would be great," he nodded. "We've had a bumpy start to our weekend."

"I can fix that," Suzie smiled.

"What? How?" Jim asked.

Just then Diana was returning to the lobby.

"Diana, seeing as you've spent extra time traveling here, we would like to make your weekend extra special so you can relax," Suzie said sympathetically. "So, I've upgraded you to the honeymoon suite."

Diana's eyes widened. "Really? The one that overlooks the water and has a spa bath and..."

"That's the one," Suzie laughed. "We're not

heavily booked, and I'd like to make sure that you both have the best vacation you can."

"This is wonderful!" she said happily.

"We'll bring your dinner and coffee to your room if you'd like," Mary offered as she returned to the lobby. "Or we could seat you on the deck, there's a nice breeze off the water."

"I think it would be nice to eat in the room tonight," Jim said with a yawn. "I'm pretty tired."

"I'll take you there, now," Mary said.

"Mary, the honeymoon suite!" Suzie called out.

"Oh?" Mary smiled. "I'm sure you'll both enjoy it, it's a huge space."

As Mary led Diana and Jim off, Suzie finally breathed a sigh of relief. Even though they only had four guests she felt as if she had run a marathon. She had a slight twinge of panic over what she might have gotten herself into. Between the troublesome Alice Montreal, the pipe problem, and the question that Paul had posed to her, she was exhausted. Luckily the intercom was set to ring to her room in case there were any problems during the night. Once everyone was settled she and Mary met up in the dining room to make sure things were ready for breakfast the next morning.

"What a day," Mary sighed as she heaved herself into a chair.

"How are you holding up?" Suzie asked.

"I'm okay, I just didn't imagine it would be so frenzied," she laughed.

"And we haven't even made breakfast yet," Suzie pointed out.

"Mom, Suzie, are you in here?" Ben called out from the lobby.

"In the dining room," Mary called back. "What's the verdict?" she asked when Ben walked in.

"Well, it's not good," Ben said grimly. "He's

got the pipes flowing for tonight, but you're losing water every time someone uses the water. You're going to have a big bill."

"What about a fix?" Suzie asked hopefully.

"He says that he can fix it," Ben said. "But he has to go into town to get some more parts and the stores won't be open until tomorrow morning. He couldn't see much under the house, but he did say it was strange that the wood was pulled back. It looks like someone pried at it."

"What?" Mary gasped. "Why would anyone do that?"

"I don't know," Suzie said grimly. "But we better keep a close eye on things until we find out."

"Thanks for your help, Ben," Mary said. "Is it okay if we just have a quiet night in tonight? I am bushed."

"That's perfect. So am I," Ben agreed. "I'll see more of Garber tomorrow. I am going out tomorrow night with Jason and his girlfriend, to check out the Garber nightlife."

"Garber has nightlife?" Mary asked.

"Jason has a girlfriend?" Suzie asked.

"I guess I'll find out tomorrow," Ben said.

"And so will we," Suzie said as she passed a glance to Mary.

Suzie stopped by Martin's room one last time, to offer him dinner, but there was still no answer. She noticed that the note under the door was now completely gone.

That night as she tried to get some rest, her thoughts turned to Paul out on his boat. She wondered what he was doing. Likely fixing up his traps and preparing for the early morning fish.

Chapter Five

Early the next morning Suzie and Mary met in the kitchen. There was breakfast to prepare for four guests. Though Suzie doubted that Martin would join them for that, Alice was there in her robe and fluffy slippers within minutes of the coffee brewing.

"That smells good," she sighed as she settled down at the dining room table.

"What do you like in your coffee?" Mary asked warmly.

"Two sugars, one cream," Alice said.

"Did you have a chance to enjoy your bath?" Suzie asked as she set a tray of fruit, danishes, and toast out on the table.

"Yes, I did," she replied. "I would have preferred if it was ready when I needed it, but I have to admit the water was toasty and the bath was beautiful."

Suzie smiled with relief. She was glad that Alice seemed to be having a better time now that she could have a bath. Now, if the plumber could get everything fixed properly she could finally feel comfortable again. She looked out the window and was relieved to see the plumber stepping out of his van. At least he would be working on fixing the problem.

"Good morning," Jim said as he and Diana walked down the hallway towards the dining room table. They were both dressed for the beach, Diana in a bathing suit, Jim in board shorts.

"Good morning," Mary said as she looked at the two of them.

"It's a lovely day for going to the beach. Feel free to take the chairs and a tent from around the back so you can enjoy the water without too much sun."

"Thank you so much," Jim said. "I have to say this place is absolutely wonderful."

"I'm glad you think so," Suzie said with a smile. "Remember we do have lunch and dinner available, but there are also several great restaurants in town you might enjoy. Cheney's is great if you like pasta, and there is also a nice diner that you can get a quick bite at."

"Great," Diana nodded. "I think we're going to spend most of the day out on the beach. Maybe we'll pick something up from the diner."

"Do you have any plans for today?" Mary asked Alice politely.

"I'll probably do a little shopping, if there is any," she said, her snooty attitude returning with force.

"Well, if any of you have any questions about Garber, or Dune House, please feel free to ask at any time," Suzie said quickly.

"Thanks, we'll do that," Jim said.

Suzie went to get herself a cup of coffee. As she stood in the kitchen she looked out over the sandy trail that led from the back of the house to the beach. She noticed that there were some footprints, and what looked like drag marks. She narrowed her eyes, wondering what had caused them. But there wasn't time to investigate as she had to get back to the guests. When she returned to the table she and Mary shared the meal with their guests. They chatted a little about Garber and then everyone went their separate ways.

After cleaning up from breakfast and preparing what she could for lunch, Suzie glanced at her watch. It was getting late, and she hadn't heard a peep from the plumber. She walked out onto the front porch. The plumber's van was still in the parking lot so she assumed he was still working. She stepped back inside and got involved in tidying up the guest rooms. She knocked lightly on Martin's door to see if anything needed cleaning.

"Martin, I'm just checking in to see if you need anything," she called out through the door. There was silence inside, and then a slight scuffing sound. The sound made her a little uneasy. She really wanted to know what he was up to in there. "Martin?" she called out again.

"I'm fine," he finally replied. "Please don't disturb me."

Suzie was surprised by his words but walked away from the door hoping she hadn't interrupted anything important.

"Suzie, have you seen the plumber?" Ben asked as he walked into the kitchen.

"No, I was just going to check on him," she replied.

"I just walked by the area where he is supposed to be working and I didn't hear a sound. I called out to him, but he didn't answer," he explained with a frown.

"What's going on?" Mary asked as she returned from tidying up the common bathroom.

"Looks like the plumber might be missing in

action," Suzie sighed. "I hope he's reliable."

"If his van's here and he's nowhere to be seen, then he's probably under the house still," Mary pointed out.

"Maybe," Ben said thoughtfully. "But he didn't answer me when I called to him."

"He might have just been getting something from his van," Mary suggested.

"Yeah, we could have just missed each other," Ben offered.

"Possibly," Suzie said. "But, we better go make sure he's not under the house. He might be hurt."

"I'll go and try call for him again," Ben said.

"I'll come, too," Mary offered.

"Let's all go together," Suzie said with a smile.

The three walked out of Dune House.

"I'll just go passed his van and make sure he isn't there," Ben offered.

"Okay, we'll meet you by the side," Suzie said as she and Mary walked towards where the plumber should have been working. There was no sign of Doug when they got there.

"Doug," Suzie crouched down and called through the opening. "Doug?" she said louder as Ben came towards them.

"No luck," Ben said as he shook his head.

"Where could he be?" Mary asked.

"Here let me try," Ben offered. "Doug? Doug are you there?" he called out. When he heard no response he crouched down. "Doug?" he called again. "I'll go see if he is in there."

"Be careful, Ben!" Mary said fretfully. Ben went on his haunches and crawled under the house.

Suzie and Mary looked at each other nervously as they waited for a response.

"Oh no, oh no!" Ben's voice bellowed from under the house and Suzie and Mary looked at each other in shock as they jumped at the sound of his worried voice. Ben scrambled out from under the house. When he got to his feet his face was white and his eyes were wide. "He's down there," he stammered out.

"What's wrong then?" Suzie asked anxiously.

"He's dead!" Ben exclaimed.

"What?" Mary gasped as she grabbed her son's hand. "Are you sure? Maybe he's just knocked out?"

"No, Mom," Ben said, his voice trembling. "I'm pretty sure," he lowered his voice. "He's dead."

"I'll call an ambulance just in case," Suzie said shakily and pulled out her cell phone. She fired off the details. She then called Jason as Mary tried to soothe Ben. He was obviously shaken up.

"Suzie, I'm going to take Ben inside," Mary said quietly. "We'll keep everyone away from this area."

"Thank you," Suzie said. "Ben, are you okay?" she asked with concern.

"I think so," he replied nervously. As Mary took Ben inside, the ambulance pulled into the driveway, it must have been only moments away when the call was made. The medics followed Suzie's directions to get to Doug and went under the house just as Jason's police car pulled up. He kept his lights and sirens off out of respect for Suzie's guests.

"What happened?" he asked as he jogged up to her. Two more police cars pulled in behind his. Suzie guessed it might have been the entire Garber police department.

"I have no idea," Suzie replied. "The plumber went under the house to do some repairs. It had been almost three hours since the last time we saw him, so we decided to go find him. Ben offered to go under the house to see if he was there. That's when he found Doug. He said that he was sure he's dead."

The medics emerged and one shook his head indicating that Doug was definitely deceased. Suzie's heart dropped as she realized that her worst fears were confirmed.

"Okay, Charlie go check it out," Jason directed one of the officers that was walking towards him. "But be careful. Don't disturb anything, it could be evidence."

When Charlie came back out from under the house his expression was grave. He held up a metal shovel that was speckled with blood.

"I've got the murder weapon," he said with confidence.

"Well, don't touch it!" Jason said with exasperation. He handed Charlie a plastic evidence bag. When he turned back to Suzie his expression was serious. "I'm going to have to talk to Ben and Mary as well as your guests, Suzie."

"Why?" Suzie asked. "I'm sure none of them had anything to do with it."

"Well, that may be but I have to find out where they were around the time of the murder so we can eliminate them as suspects," he rested his hand on the side of his gun belt and looked very determined.

"I know you're just doing your job, Jason," Suzie said quietly. A man was dead, and now her guests would be subjected to a police investigation. It was not the bumps she expected on an opening weekend. "I'll get you their information."

As the two stepped into Dune House, Alice was entering through the side sliding door. She had said she was going shopping, but she was dressed for the beach.

"Alice, could I speak with you for a moment?" Suzie asked as she blocked her from walking down the hallway towards her room.

"What is it?" Alice asked as she glanced towards Jason. She winked lightly at him when she caught him looking at her tiny bikini.

"There's been an unfortunate incident, and I'm afraid the police will need to question all of the guests," Suzie explained hesitantly.

"What kind of unfortunate incident?" Alice demanded to know. "Did somebody die or something?"

"Actually, yes," Suzie replied with a frown. "The plumber that was working under the house, was killed."

"Great, just great," Alice rolled her eyes. Suzie winced at her lack of sympathy but she said nothing about it.

"It's just routine in situations like this to find out where everyone was around the time we estimate the death occurred," Jason explained. Suzie could tell that he was trying his best to play down the event for the sake of the B & B, but she also knew that he had a job that he had to do.

"Oh, this is ridiculous," Alice said with a sharp

shake of her head. "It's none of your business where I was or what I was doing. I am here on vacation," she added with building frustration.

"And I want you to get back to that vacation as soon as you can," Jason offered in a docile tone. "But I can't do that unless you can confirm to me your whereabouts."

Alice blew out a breath of air through her nose and crossed her arms.

"All you need to know is that I had nothing to do with any of this. Any other questions I'm not answering without a lawyer present," she insisted.

Jason glanced over at Suzie briefly and then back to Alice.

"This really will be over with if you just answer a few of my questions," Jason attempted to persuade her.

"I'm not answering any more questions," Alice said sternly. "In fact, I expect a full refund for my stay here this weekend," she added and looked pointedly at Suzie.

Suzie narrowed her eyes. She was doing her best not to lose her cool, but Alice was really pushing it. Since she and Mary had already discussed offering their guests a complimentary stay in the future, she wasn't opposed to the refund, but Alice's attitude and refusal to cooperate was really grating on her nerves.

"Here is my card," Jason said as he handed her a business card. "When you get in contact with your lawyer, have him contact me."

Alice took the card begrudgingly. Then she turned and walked away with a flick of her long, dark hair.

"She's rather difficult," Jason said grimly when Alice was out of earshot.

"The question is why is she being so difficult?" Suzie mused with a frown. She was beginning to think that Alice might just be hiding something.

"Honestly, her evasiveness makes her look

pretty suspicious," Jason admitted. "We'll look into her and see if she has any connections to Doug."

Suzie nodded. She felt queasy. She wanted to believe that none of the guests at Dune House had any involvement with Doug's death.

"Hello?" a timid voice called out that Suzie recognized as Jim's.

"Jim and Diana must be back," she said to Jason. "Hopefully, they'll be more forthcoming."

Jason and Suzie walked out into the lobby where Jim and a very sunburned Diana were glancing around apprehensively.

"What's going on?" Diana asked when she saw Suzie. "Why are the police here?"

"Unfortunately, there's been a death on the property," Suzie explained carefully.

"I just need to ask you a few questions about where you both were this morning when the death occurred," Jason added.

"A death?" Jim stumbled out. "Who was it? Not any of the guests or staff I hope?"

"No," Suzie shook her head, and then let Jason take over.

"It was a plumber who was working under the house on some pipes," Jason explained. "Can you tell me where you were today?"

Diana sighed and pointed to her crimson skin. "I fell asleep on the beach."

"I was swimming," Jim frowned. "We've been on the beach since after breakfast."

"Okay, and did you notice anyone suspicious around Dune House at any time during your stay?" he asked as he made a note.

"No one other than that strange fellow in the suit," Jim replied. "I saw him walking down to the beach and waved hello, but he just hurried off back towards the house."

"He wasn't suspicious, just different," Diana corrected him. "He just wasn't very friendly."

"So, is this a murder?" Jim pressed. "Should we be concerned about our safety?"

"No, there's no need for that," Jason said firmly. "This seems to have been a targeted crime, and there will be a police presence while we investigate."

"It's still pretty creepy," Diana whispered.

"I understand," Suzie nodded. "I'm sure this was not what you expected to happen on your weekend away, however it has happened and I am sure that the police will get to the bottom of it. I would like to offer you a complimentary stay at some point in the future, if you would be interested."

"Well," Jim said slowly. "It's not your fault this happened. No one can predict these things."

As the couple walked down the hall towards their room Suzie felt some relief that they had not been as difficult as Alice.

Chapter Six

There was only one guest left for Jason to speak to. Hopefully, he would prove more obliging than Alice but Suzie doubted that that would be the case.

"I still have to speak with Martin Cotes," Jason said as he turned to Suzie. "Any idea where he might be?"

"As far as I know he hasn't left his room," Suzie replied. "He didn't show up for lunch today. Other than Jim and Diana seeing him outside, I haven't heard of anyone seeing him."

"That's a little odd isn't it?" Jason asked thoughtfully.

"He is a little odd," Suzie pointed out. "He brought all kinds of equipment with him, I'm not sure what it's for. I assumed he's working on some kind of project."

"Well, let's go and see if he's in his room,"

Jason suggested. The two walked towards the room that was still closed up tight. Mary came down the stairs as they did.

"Ben is beside himself," she said with a sigh. "He's never seen anything like this before."

"I'll need to talk to him, too," Jason said quickly. "But we can give him a few minutes to regain his composure."

"Good, thank you, Jason," Mary said. Jason and Suzie continued on to Martin's room.

When Suzie and Jason got to Martin's room Suzie felt a bit uneasy. She could not believe that someone had been murdered at Dune house. She steadied her breath as Jason knocked heavily on the door to Martin's room. When he received no answer he tried the handle.

"It's locked,' he said. "Suzie, do you have a key to the room?"

"I do," she nodded. "But do you think it's right to barge in?"

"Well, with one person dead on the property we need to make sure at the very least that everyone is accounted for and not hurt."

"You're right," Suzie nodded. She reached into her pocket and retrieved a small key ring. She stepped past Jason and slid a key into the door knob. She turned it and twisted the knob at the same time. As the door swung open she braced herself. She had no idea what they might find inside. Would Martin be hurt or worse? Would he even be inside?

"Excuse me, Mr. Cotes?" Jason called out as he stepped in behind Suzie. It was clear that he was there, as he was sitting at the small table with a pair of headphones on. That explained why he hadn't answered the door, he could not hear the knock. When he glanced up to see Suzie and Jason standing inside the door he jumped.

"What are you doing in here?" Martin demanded. "I asked not to be disturbed."

"I'm very sorry, Mr. Cotes, but this police officer needs to ask you a few questions. There was a murder on the property."

"That's terrible," he said as he edged closer towards the equipment piled on the floor.

"What's all this?" Jason asked.

"It's just some things I brought along with me," Martin shrugged. "Beach combing, that kind of thing."

Suzie raised an eyebrow. She wondered how he could have been beach combing if he had rarely left the room.

"Ah, I see," Jason nodded but he was still looking skeptically at the equipment. "Well, all I need to know is where you were today."

"Oh I, well," Martin pushed his glasses further up. He looked over at Suzie, as if she might have the answer. "I was here, most of the day," he explained.

"Jim said he saw you out by the beach," Suzie

volunteered. Jason shot her a dark look of warning. Suzie realized she might have overstepped the mark.

"Oh right, yes, I was out on the beach, but only for a few minutes. It's just so hot," he added.

"Can you tell me if you noticed anyone else around the building? Or maybe out on the beach?" Jason asked.

"I did see that other woman that's staying here. Alice I think her name is. She was poking all around the house," Martin explained. "I saw her looking under the porch and such. I thought it was a little odd."

"Thank you," Jason said as he put away his notepad. "You've been very helpful."

As they stepped out of the room, Jason turned to look at Suzie.

"You have to let me ask the questions, and let the guests answer on their own," he said firmly.

"I'm sorry, Jason, I didn't mean to interfere,"

Suzie cringed at the thought of affecting one of Jason's investigations.

Mary walked towards them and stood silently in the hall, looking between the two.

"I know," he nodded, but his expression was still dark. "I'm going to check in with the department and make sure we can get a rush on the forensics. The body should be removed soon."

Suzie closed her eyes at the mention of 'the body'. "Poor Doug," she said softly. Mary gave Suzie's shoulder a light squeeze.

"Yes," Jason nodded. "Oh Mary, can you have Ben meet me at the station when he's ready so I can ask him some questions?"

"I'll let him know," Mary promised. Jason returned to the other officers investigating the scene. Mary grimaced as she guided Suzie towards the dining room.

"This is some mess we have on our hands," Suzie sighed

"It sure is," Mary agreed. "From the sound of it, there are no suspects. But who could have killed Doug? It makes no sense!"

"Martin said something about Alice snooping around. Why would she be doing that if she had nothing to do with this?" Suzie asked.

"That's a good point," Mary agreed. "She must be up to something. But I have a hard time believing that she would sneak under the house."

"Maybe, but she was laying it on pretty thick, wasn't she? With her spoiled attitude? Maybe it was all a farce to throw us off," Suzie suggested.

"You know we could say the same about anyone," Mary sighed. "I think the key to all of this, is why. Why did someone kill the plumber? If someone had a personal vendetta, there were plenty of easier ways to handle it. Why would they wait until they had to crawl under a house to do it?"

"Maybe that's it," Suzie suddenly gasped.

"What if it has nothing to do with the plumber?"

"What are you talking about, Suzie?" Mary shook her head. "Of course it's about the plumber, he's the one that's dead."

"But think about it," Suzie said quickly. "Someone was trying to get under the house before the plumber ever arrived."

"So, if it wasn't about the plumber, if the plumber just happened to be in the wrong place at the wrong time, then what was it about?" Mary said softly. "I mean, there is nothing under Dune House but pipes."

"Remember that Doug said it looked like someone had intentionally damaged the pipe. We thought maybe it was one of the locals," Suzie said as she sat back in her chair. "But now that I think about it, I don't think anyone local would have done this. Why go to all the trouble of damaging a pipe when they could have just broken windows or even started a fire?"

"You're right," Mary nodded. "So, why would someone have damaged the pipes on purpose?"

"Here's the thing," Suzie said in a whisper. "At this point it could have been anyone. The key is knowing exactly what they might have been doing under the house."

"If it wasn't intentional sabotage, then it must have been something else," Mary narrowed her eyes. "For someone to go to all the trouble of risking getting caught, as well as killing another person, then they must have had a very good reason for going under the house."

"I think we should do a little research," Suzie suggested. "Maybe there is something about Dune House that we don't know."

Mary's eyes widened. "You know, Ben said he thought he saw someone walking around the house. But when he went outside no one was there. Maybe that person went under the house," her face paled with fear. "To think that my son could have been that close to a murderer."

"I'm sorry, Mary. That must be a terrible thought," Suzie grimaced. "But I think you're right. Ben did see someone, and that person probably did go under the house. So, even before our guests arrived, something strange was going on here."

"If it's none of the guests, then it had to be someone local. We need to get to the bottom of this," she said sternly.

"Yes, we do," Suzie agreed. "I know just the person to ask."

"You do?" Mary asked with surprise.

"Louis, the librarian," Suzie said. "He knows more about this little town, and this house, than either of us put together."

"Why don't you pay him a visit, and I'll stay here to look after the guests?" Mary suggested. "I want to talk to Ben about what he saw, and let him know that he needs to meet Jason at the police station."

"Are you sure?" Suzie asked. "I don't want to leave you with too much to handle."

"Don't worry about me," Mary insisted. "I can handle it," she said with confidence. Suzie was sure Mary could handle it, but she wasn't sure if she would be able to handle finding out the truth about Dune House. What if one of its secrets was so terrible that she wouldn't be able to continue to live in it?

Chapter Seven

As Suzie drove towards the library she wished that Paul was on land. He would help her sort through things. He was very intelligent, something that Suzie respected deeply about him. But he was out at sea, and likely wouldn't be back until the next day. So, she had no choice but to try to piece things together herself. She parked in the nearly empty parking lot and walked up to the library. There were a few people inside, but not too many. The librarian behind the desk smiled at her as she walked in.

"Hi Louis," Suzie smiled.

"Hi Suzie," Louis said. "How is opening weekend going?"

"Oh well, it's going," Suzie said casually. She didn't want the whole town knowing about the murder just yet. "I was wondering if I could tap into some of your knowledge about Garber's history."

"Anything for you," he said with a slight smile. Suzie wasn't sure if he meant it, but she was happy he was willing to help her.

"What can you tell me about the history of Dune House, anything that involves something under the house?" Suzie asked hopefully.

"There is so much history with Dune House," Louis said as he pulled his glasses off and began to polish them with the hem of his shirt. "But as for something being under it," he hummed thoughtfully and put his glasses back on. "I only know of one thing involving that."

"What?" Suzie asked, trying not to hold her breath.

"Well, a long time ago just as the civil war was moving through the area, Dune House was supposed to be used as the governor's mansion. It was renovated and filled to the hilt with luxuries. Unfortunately, before the governor could even move into it, the civil war shifted and fighting began in Garber."

"Oh," Suzie said with a slight shake of her head. She was trying to be attentive but she didn't see how any of that had anything to do with something under the house.

"In the midst of all the fighting, a few of the governor's men were rumored to have made an effort to protect his riches. They piled everything of value into a solid chest and buried it under the house. Supposedly, gold, jewels, even a rare painting or two. For a little while after the fighting moved on, it became like a local fable. The riches by the sea. But no one dared to look for it, because the governor still owned the house and he threatened to murder anyone who stepped on his property. There were rumors of a few people attempting to search for the riches, but they didn't turn up anything."

"So, no one ever found the valuables?" Suzie asked with surprise. "It could still be under there?"

"Of course not," Louis laughed. "If there was gold, it was found, I can promise you that."

"How do you know?" Suzie asked.

"The house changed hands a few years later. They renovated the house again, and did their best to repair all of the damage that had been done by the fighting. The rumor persisted for a little while, before it just died out."

"Huh," Suzie said thoughtfully. "And that's the only information you have about something hidden under the house?"

"Yes, no buried bodies, no secrets," he shrugged.

"That must be it then," Suzie said softly. "Someone was trying to find that gold."

"Well, that would be a pipe dream, I mean think about it. If it was the governor's men who hid the gold, the governor would have demanded they retrieve it," he explained. "The pipes in that

118

old place had to have been redone at least three times. I'm sure that someone would have stumbled across hidden money if it was still there."

Suzie nodded. "Thank you, Louis, you've been very helpful."

"Well, I try," he smiled. "Now, as to the other stories about Dune House..."

"Another day," Suzie said with a polite smile. "I have to get back to my guests. Thank you again, Louis."

"Anytime," he nodded as he turned back to the pile of magazines he had been sorting through.

Suzie's mind was spinning as she drove back to Dune House. She was now very suspicious of one guest in particular. When she arrived Mary was sweeping the front porch. There was no sign of any of the guests.

"Where is everyone?" Suzie asked as she

hurried up onto the porch.

"Alice went into town, Jim and Diana took a pamphlet for the local museum," Mary replied and rested the broom against the outside wall of the house.

"And Martin?" Suzie asked, narrowing her eyes. "Have you seen him?"

"As far as I know he's still in his room," Mary shrugged.

"I think we need to be very careful about that," Suzie said. "I think he's the one that was under the house."

"What? Why do you think that?" Mary asked with a frown.

"Because there was once a rumor that there was gold and other valuables hidden under the house," Suzie explained. "With all of that equipment that he had I bet he was using that to figure out exactly where the gold might be hidden."

"Do you think he was involved with Doug's murder?" Mary asked in a hushed voice.

"I don't know," Suzie replied nervously. "But I think that we need to be extra cautious around him."

"Have you spoken to Jason about it?" she asked as she stepped closer to Suzie.

"Spoken to me about what?" Jason asked as he stepped out of his patrol car. Suzie was startled by his sudden presence as she hadn't even heard the car pull up. Ben was with him, and climbed the steps up to the porch to stand next to his mother.

"I'll let her tell you," Mary said as she looked over at Ben. "I want to talk to you in private, please."

Ben raised an eyebrow as if he was instinctively wondering if he was in trouble. Once Mary and Ben had stepped off the porch and into the house Suzie turned to face Jason.

"I need to talk to you about Martin Cotes," she

said quickly. Jason held up a hand to silence her.

"Listen Suzie, I found out some information about Alice Montreal," Jason said as he leaned back against the porch railing.

"What is it?" Suzie asked curiously. "Does she have a criminal past?"

"No, not criminal," he replied. "She runs a B & B in the next town."

"What?" Suzie asked with surprise. "She must have come here to check out the competition."

"Must have," Jason agreed. "It doesn't make her a killer."

"No, it doesn't," Suzie agreed. "But she might have been the one that damaged the pipe in the first place. Maybe she went under the house to cause more problems and Doug caught her. If he did, then maybe she panicked."

"It's possible," Jason said and cringed. "But she doesn't look like she's ever had a trace of dirt on her. Somehow it's hard for me to believe that she wiggled her way under the house."

"Ah Jason," Suzie said sweetly. "You're still young. Just because a woman is pretty, doesn't mean she's not capable of terrible things."

"I know that," Jason said gruffly and then rubbed his chin slowly. "But it still doesn't quite add up to me."

"We might not know exactly who yet, but I have another idea as to why," Suzie said. "I visited the library today to talk to Louis about the history of Dune House. He told me a story about gold and other valuables being hidden under the house during the civil war. I believe that whoever went under the house went under looking for that gold."

"Well, that's a theory," Jason said hesitantly. "But that was so long ago. Who would even have that knowledge?"

"Maybe Martin Cotes," she pointed out. "He knew that the bannister on the porch was not the original. He seemed very interested in the history of the house. He also has strange tools and equipment in his room."

"Plenty of people will stay here because they are interested in the history of the house, and those that do will probably know some of the history of the house. Besides, Martin explained to us that he was using the equipment on the beach for beach combing. Do you know how many tourists and locals do the same thing?" he shook his head. "That's not enough reason to suspect a man of murder."

Suzie nodded. "I guess you're right. I was a little quick to judge. It would make a lot more sense if this was simple competition issues with another B & B. Alice was poking around the outside of the house. She probably damaged the pipe to make us look bad. Maybe she was under the house to do more damage when the plumber caught her."

"It is a solid lead for right now. I want to see if

I can catch up with her," he suggested.

"Yes, I'd love to see what she has to say for herself," Suzie said. As they walked into the house, Suzie could hear Ben and Mary talking in the kitchen. It sounded like Mary was warning him about Martin. Suzie made a mental note to speak to her about Alice. Just as she had the thought Alice walked in through the front door. She glanced between Jason and Suzie and then walked past them.

Suzie moved to chase after her, but Jason held her back.

"Wait, give her a moment. I don't want to spook her."

"But she might not come back out of her room," Suzie pointed out impatiently.

"She will, she's too curious not to," Jason said with confidence. Jason's cell phone rang, "I have to get this," he said as he walked towards the front door.

After a few minutes Jason still hadn't returned and Alice was back dressed in her bathing suit and walking casually towards the side door that led to the beach.

Suzie didn't want the opportunity to pass as she wanted to talk to her.

"Alice," she said firmly. "Can I talk to you for a second, please?"

"I don't have time to talk," Alice smiled sweetly and attempted to dodge around Suzie.

"It will only take a minute," Suzie said as Alice tried to slip passed her to head out to the beach.

"What?" Alice asked as she glared at Suzie.

"I know who you are, Alice," Suzie said calmly.

"I should hope so," Alice replied. "I'm your guest."

"You run a B & B of your own, don't you?"

Alice frowned. "So, what if I do?"

"So, maybe you came here to see what Dune House offered," Suzie pointed out.

"And?" Alice asked and flipped her long, dark hair. "That's not a crime the last time I checked."

"No, it isn't," Suzie agreed. Suzie saw Jason walk back into Dune House and straight over to Alice.

"I haven't heard from your lawyer yet, Ms. Montreal," Jason said in a stern voice. "Maybe it's time you really called one. Because there is evidence building up that you might have had something to do with this and if you didn't I imagine you would want to clear your name."

"Well, the evidence that you're both certifiably insane is building up pretty fast as well," she growled as she glared at both of them.

"Are you denying that you are here because I am your competition?" Suzie asked.

"Ha, you think this is competition?" she demanded. "You have no idea what you're talking about. My bed and breakfast is beautiful. It has a hot tub, it has breakfast in bed, this place is a dingy old dump compared to it," she said arrogantly as she turned on her heal and pranced out onto the beach, as if she didn't have a care in the world.

"Why didn't you arrest her?" Suzie looked over at Jason

"I don't have enough evidence," he said in a low voice. "I have to let her go."

"I can't believe you just let her go," Suzie said with frustration.

"Suzie, I can't just arrest everyone I see," Jason countered with reflected irritation.

"Can you arrest a murderer?" she demanded.

"What's all this shouting about?" Martin asked from the hallway.

Suzie fell silent as she turned to look in his direction. Jason looked towards him as well. Martin stood perfectly still in the entrance of the hallway. Now, that Suzie had another look at him, he really did seem harmless. Dressed carefully in his fancy suit, he didn't look like the type to go digging around underneath a house. Her eyes dropped down to his shoes, where she noticed no trace of dirt caked on them. In fact his shoes looked spotless.

"Sorry, to have disturbed you, Martin," Suzie said calmly.

"Well, it's hard not to be disturbed when I hear all of this shouting and carrying on," Martin said grimly. "First you violate my privacy by coming into my room with a police officer. Now, I can't even do my research in peace."

"What research would that be?" Jason asked, not bothered by the man's accusations.

"I don't have to tell you that," Martin said stubbornly.

"No, of course you don't," Suzie said with a short laugh. "It's not like you're under investigation or something. But we were just curious what you have been up to. It must be something very interesting for you to spend so much of your time on it."

"Well," Martin sighed. "If you must know, I am working on very interesting research. I am trying to study the level of metals in the sand at area beaches. People never discuss the dangers of sand, but they should. If the heavy metals are in the sand, then they are in our environment much more frequently than we believe."

"That's impressive," Suzie said.

"I have never thought about that," Mary added quietly. Ben nodded beside her.

"There's nothing wrong with Garber sand," Jason said defensively. "We've always kept the beach pristine."

"Always?" Martin asked. "Even after the civil war when most of the town was burned to the ground? Do you really think people were concerned about what was tossed or leaked into the water then?"

Suzie tensed at the mention of the civil war. If he knew about the civil war moving through Garber then he likely had read about the gold that was rumored to be hidden there. But his explanation about testing the sand explained his equipment.

"Maybe not," Jason said quietly. "But the water is tested frequently to ensure its safety."

"And the sand?" Martin pressed. "When was the last time that you had the sand tested?"

"No one has ever tested the sand," Jason admitted. "That I know of."

"Well, then you can see how important my research is," Martin said with confidence. "No one thinks things through. If the sand is part of our eco-system, it matters. It impacts animals, humans, food supply, everything you can think of."

"I guess it's a good thing that you're testing it then," Jason said calmly. "It's a lot better than what I've known treasure hunters to do to the beach. They like to dig holes looking for gold," he paused at that and seemed to be studying Martin's face intently.

"There is nothing worse than a misguided treasure hunter," Martin announced with disgust in his voice. "If any of them knew the truth, that the only treasure we have is this earth, then they wouldn't waste so much time trying to find gold," he shook his head.

Suzie bit into her bottom lip. She glanced over at Mary, who looked over at Ben. Suzie was finding Martin less and less suspicious by the moment.

"I'd have to agree with you there," Jason admitted as his gaze lingered on Martin. His expression was stolid, not revealing a hint of what he was thinking or feeling.

"How can you test the sand if you never leave your room?" Suzie questioned.

"Oh," Martin cleared his throat. "Well, I got a sample when I first arrived and I've been doing tests on it using the equipment in my room ever since."

"Oh, okay," Suzie said casually but she noticed that Martin looked a bit nervous.

"If you'll excuse me, I need to get back to my research," he said sternly.

"Of course. We'll try not to disturb you again," Suzie said apologetically.

"Please, try your hardest," Martin requested with a bite to his words. Then he turned and calmly walked back to his room. He shut his door with a sharp slam.

Mary looked over at Suzie. "I don't think that this is going well," she said with a sigh. "Is it good business to have your guests suspected of murder?"

"I don't think so," Ben cringed.

"Well, we have to get to the bottom of this," Suzie said with exasperation. "The guests will all be leaving soon, and that might just include the murderer."

"Suzie, I need to speak with you for a moment," Jason said. Then he nodded to Mary and Ben. "Ben, I'll meet you tonight, okay?"

"Yes, I'll be there," Ben nodded.

As Suzie and Jason stepped back out on the porch, he ran a hand across his face and sighed.

"Are you okay, Jason?" Suzie asked.

"Not really," he said as he shook his head. "I need you to stop interrogating the guests."

"I know I'm sorry, Jason," Suzie said. "I just wanted to confront Alice about spying."

"I know," he nodded. "I feel like I'm getting nowhere fast on this case, and you're right, I'm running out of time."

"Well, it's not an easy case," Suzie said kindly,

"But it should be open and shut," Jason insisted. "I'm under a lot of pressure to get this solved. Doug worked a few towns over but a lot of the residents here knew him. My boss wants this solved, yesterday. But I don't want to rush the investigation, make a wrong move and end up letting the killer go free or worse, arresting an innocent person."

"You'll find the culprit," Suzie said with confidence.

"So far I have a murder with zero credible suspects and no evidence," Jason sighed and scratched his head. "I've been focusing mainly on the guests at Dune House, but really it could have been anyone in Garber at the time. Maybe it wasn't even one of the guests. Sure we suspected Alice, but she has a plausible reason for her behavior, as does Martin. I've only got Jim and Diana left, and they seem like harmless people."

"They do," Suzie agreed. "But I am sure it has to be either Alice or Martin."

"Except I have zero evidence to support either accusation," Jason pointed out morosely.

"Wait, you do have one piece of evidence," Suzie pointed out. "The shovel."

"Oh yes," he nodded. "And that will be great once we have a suspect. The blood on it belonged to the victim. There were no usable fingerprints. It looked almost brand new but it is useless to us."

"That's not very helpful is it?" Suzie sighed.

"No and James from Winston's has been away the last couple of days so I couldn't ask him if Doug bought the shovel, his assistant couldn't help us at all, he wasn't working the day Doug went in there, presuming that he even did. I don't expect it to be much help once I speak to him anyway," Jason explained. James was the owner of Winston's the hardware store in town. It always had some kind of sale happening. Suzie had loved going there while she was fixing up Dune House. "Anyway, I better head off. I'm going to check on some of the forensic evidence to see if they've come up with any hint as to who was under the house," Jason said.

"You're doing a good job, Jason, keep it up."

He looked up at Suzie, a little startled by her words. "Thanks Suzie," he said. "I just hope I find the murderer quickly."

She nodded as he walked towards his car.

When Jason had left Suzie looked out over the water thinking about the shovel. Why would a plumber need a shovel under the house? The pipes are not under the ground. What could he have needed it for?

She decided to go and see if James, who she had come to know quite well, was back at work and remembered who had bought it. It was probably Doug who had bought it but maybe it was his murderer.

***

The town was bustling and Suzie had to navigate to find a parking spot near Winston's which was located on the main strip of town. All of the small stores were connected by one roof on each block and very few had their own parking lots. She finally found a place to park, and hoped that the store wouldn't already be closed. Luckily the door was still unlocked when she reached it. When she walked into the store she smiled at James.

"Hi there, Suzie," he said as he walked around the counter to greet her.

"How was your time off?" she asked politely.

"Great, I was away at my cabin," he replied. "It is good to see you again. How is everything at Dune House?"

"Well, we're in a bit of a crisis," Suzie

admitted. "I was hoping that you could help me with something."

"What is it?" he asked curiously.

Suzie glanced down the aisle that sold digging tools. "Do you have any shovels for sale?"

"Plenty," he nodded and led her down the aisle. Suzie spotted the shovel that had been recovered at the scene. It looked identical to the murder weapon.

"Do you remember selling one of these shovels to anyone lately?" Suzie asked hopefully.

"Ah, well," he narrowed his eyes slightly. "It's hard to say, I honestly don't always pay attention."

"Maybe you could check your records," Suzie suggested. "Your receipts?"

"Actually," he took the shovel from Suzie. "I know for sure I sold at least one. I'm just not sure if I sold more than one."

"Do you remember who you sold it to?" Suzie asked eagerly. "Do you have security cameras?"

"No, I don't have cameras. I don't like those new-fangled things. I think you should give people the benefit of the doubt, not videotape them just for walking through your door," he sighed. "But I do remember who I sold it to. Yes, now it's coming back to me. The man who bought this type of shovel was dressed funny. He said he was staying at Dune House. It just struck me as odd, because if you're staying at a B & B why would you need a shovel?"

Suzie bit her tongue instead of telling him exactly what he had needed it for. So, it was Martin who had bought the shovel. The murder weapon.

"Yes, strange fellow, it was about three days ago," he continued.

"Wait, three days ago?" Suzie asked. That was before Martin had arrived at Dune House. "Are you sure about that?"

"Yup, I'm sure," he nodded. "I've been away since then and I wouldn't forget that guy for anything."

"Was that all he bought?" Suzie asked.

"No, actually he also bought a pair of those slipcovers that go over your shoes to protect carpets. I have no idea what he was planning on using those for. Was he working in your garden or something?" he asked.

"No, but thank you for this information," Suzie said with a grim frown. As she turned to leave the hardware store, she knew once and for all that Martin was her main suspect. Now the only question was, would she be able to find him and stop him before he killed again?

Chapter Eight

When Suzie returned to Dune House, she had an eerie feeling. Martin's dusty car was still parked in the driveway. She pulled out her cell phone and placed a call to Jason.

"Suzie," Jason answered. Suzie decided that she was going to have to bend the truth a bit so it didn't look like she was stepping on Jason's toes.

"I went to Winston's to pick something up today and I happened to ask him about the shovel," Suzie said quickly before Jason could interrupt her. "I found out that the shovel was sold three days ago to Martin Cotes. I'm standing outside Dune House right now, and his car is still here. Can you get here soon?"

"I'll be there in a few minutes. Don't go into the house until I get there," he warned.

"But Mary is in there," Suzie argued.

"If you can get her attention, get her to come out, otherwise you're just going to have to sit tight until I get there. It will be much more dangerous if Martin suspects we're onto him. So just try to be casual. If you see him, keep your distance and be polite."

"I'll try," Suzie said fretfully. After she hung up the phone she tried to follow Jason's instructions. She really did. But all she kept thinking of was whether Martin might already have hurt Mary, or if she could be hurt before Jason arrived. Finally, she couldn't wait any longer. She crept up the steps and onto the porch. She slipped inside the house as quietly as she could. She spotted Mary in the kitchen washing some dishes.

"Mary," she hissed.

Mary looked up and over at Suzie. Her eyes narrowed as she studied her strange expression.

"What is it?" she asked.

"Come outside with me," Suzie said and gestured to the door.

"I just have a few dishes to finish up," she said and turned the water back on.

"No, Mary, no, come with me now," Suzie insisted and started walking across the dining room towards her. Just then Suzie heard a door in the hallway open. Her heart skipped a beat. She locked eyes with Mary. Mary could now clearly see the fear in Suzie's eyes.

"Suzie, what's wrong?" she asked as she moved towards her.

"Yes, Suzie what's wrong?" a voice asked from the hallway. Suzie spun on her heel to face the voice. It was a relief to see that it was Alice.

"Alice, I suggest you go out on the town today," Suzie said quickly. Then she grabbed Mary's hand. "Let's go outside ladies, it's such a nice day."

In the distance Suzie heard a scraping sound.

She couldn't be sure if it was coming from inside or outside the house.

"That's already what I was planning to do, but thanks for the tip," Alice said with a roll of her eyes. "You get stranger every time I see you."

Suzie ignored her words. All she cared about was getting the two of them out of the house before Martin emerged from his room, if he was even in there in the first place.

"Let's go outside now," she said in what she hoped was a cheerful voice. If Martin was listening in, she didn't want him to think that there was a problem. As she made her way towards the front door, she heard the scraping sound again. She still wasn't sure what the sound was, but she wasn't going to hang around to find out. Just as they stepped out onto the porch Jason's patrol car was pulling into the driveway. He jumped out of the car and jogged across the driveway to meet them at the bottom of the porch.

"I told you not to go inside," Jason barked sharply and gestured for them to move away from the porch.

"What is all of this about?" Alice demanded. "You know what, never mind," she shook her head. "I'm out of here."

She walked to her car and drove off ignoring the entire situation. Jason pulled out his radio to call for backup.

"We need to get in there and see if he's there," Suzie insisted. "If we wait for backup he could be long gone by the time they get here."

"I'll go in," Jason said firmly. "You two stay out here," he looked from Mary to Suzie and back again. "I mean it."

"We will," Mary assured him. But Suzie didn't say a word. As soon as Jason stepped through the door into Dune House, Suzie was on the move. She was afraid that if Jason went in through the front door, then Martin would go out through the side door. She ran around the porch to the side of the house.

"Suzie, where are you going?" Mary demanded as she chased after her.

"Look," Suzie said as she pointed to the window of Martin's room. It looks like someone has pushed the screen out.

"He's not in here," Jason said as he opened the window. "We must have missed him."

"Now what?" Suzie frowned as she waited for Jason to make his way back out of the house.

"Now, we have to figure out where he might have gone," Jason said as he glanced towards the beach.

"His car is still here," Mary pointed out.

"And all of his fancy equipment is still in his room," Jason frowned.

"Maybe we missed something under the house," Suzie said with a slight frown. "There has to be some clue or evidence there that was overlooked. Maybe there will be a clue of where he is. He must have been sneaking out the window all of this time that we thought he was holed up in his room. That's why the note that Mary left was pushed halfway out from under the door. The breeze from the window being opened must have made it scoot. He purchased footies to go over his shoes at the hardware store, too. He must have done that to keep from tracking dirt and sand into the room, so that we'd have no idea what he was up to," she sighed. "He really covered his bases. But I'm willing to bet if he was foolish enough to leave the shovel under the house after killing Doug that he left something else behind, too."

"It's possible," Jason admitted and adjusted his gun belt. "It is a tight space under there. I'll take a second look."

"I can't believe he just took off and left some of his equipment behind," Mary said. "It seemed so important to him when he arrived. Maybe he didn't leave at all."

"But if he didn't leave, where is he?" Suzie asked. "His car is still here. Where could he be hiding?"

"Wait a minute," Jason frowned. "If Martin is our prime suspect, then it's possible that he is still looking for that gold. If he wanted it so badly that it drove him to kill someone, would he really be willing to abandon the idea of finding it?"

"It's worth a look," Mary said nervously.

"It would be a huge risk for him to take," Suzie pointed out.

"True," Jason argued. "He couldn't have gone far. He probably felt very confident about throwing us off his scent with that speech about contaminated sand. He might have taken another chance," he lowered his voice. "He could still very well be underneath Dune House."

"Let's find out," Suzie said boldly. Mary nodded her agreement.

"I guess it would do no good to ask you two to stay here out of harm's way?" Jason asked grimly.

"You can always ask," Suzie said sweetly. Mary only shook her head.

"Fine, you can come with me, but stay back from the house. If Martin is down there, he's going to be desperate when he is caught," he frowned and adjusted his gun in the holster. Suzie noticed that he made sure that the strap that secured it was loosened.

Carefully the three of them walked around to the side of the house. Jason put his finger to his lips, motioning for them to be as quiet as possible. It was clear that someone had been there recently as the pile of dirt that had been removed in order to give the police easier access to the space had been disturbed and the crime scene tape had been torn. Jason crouched down slowly, doing his best to be silent. Suzie and Mary stayed close together as Jason peered into the opening.

He glanced back over his shoulder at Mary and Suzie. His eyebrow raised and he gave a slight nod. He reached down and turned off his radio to make sure he could move in total quiet. As he crept beneath the house he drew his gun.

"Don't move!" he barked out. Suzie and Mary looked at each other and braced themselves for a potential gunshot. "Stop!" Jason shouted. They could hear scuffling and groaning from under the house.

Suzie stood near the edge of the entrance. She wondered if she should go inside to help or not. A moment later Jason backed out from under the house, dragging Martin with him. Martin was already handcuffed.

"How did you do that?" Suzie asked, obviously impressed.

Martin was sputtering dirt from his mouth and it looked as if Jason had given him a solid punch to the side of his face.

Jason was out of breath as he held tightly to Martin. It was clear that they had wrestled quite a bit below the house.

"I don't know to be honest," Jason gasped out. "But it's done."

"What are you doing!" Martin exclaimed.

"You're under arrest," Jason said breathlessly.

"For what?" Martin questioned.

"For murder!" Jason explained.

"But I didn't do anything," Martin raised his voice.

"We know that you purchased the shovel," Jason said. "The murder weapon."

"So what?" he said with a shrug.

"Well, why would you need a shovel and be snooping around a crime scene?" Jason asked. Martin seemed lost for words as he was contemplating what to say next. His eyes seemed to sparkle as something occurred to him.

"Oh, all right," Martin said as he sighed. "But, I'm this close to finding a fortune. This can just be between us," he offered. "I'll share the gold with all of you."

Suzie, Mary and Jason stared at him in astonishment. He wasn't just weird he was loony.

"Why did you murder him?" Jason asked trying to get as much information from him before he declined his offer of sharing the gold. Martin seemed to think that they were still going to accept the offer.

"I didn't mean to," Martin replied matter-of-factly. "I was looking for the gold, our gold," he said with a smile. "I accidently damaged the pipe and then when I was looking for it again Doug came down and saw me. He wanted to know what I was doing and when I told him he said he was going to tell the police."

"So you decided to kill him," Jason said in

astonishment.

"I had no choice. I offered to share it with him but he didn't want a bar of it," Martin explained. "I couldn't let all my hard work be for nothing. I was so close. I am so close."

"You did a terrible thing, for nothing. There's no gold under that house. There hasn't been gold under there for decades. What was there was either found or moved. You killed someone for nothing," Jason said in disbelief.

"What?" Martin stammered out. "But I've done my research. I know that it's true. I've looked into it for years."

"You were wrong," Suzie said sternly. "And you took the life of a good man because of it."

Martin fell silent. His glasses were smudged with dirt and had slid down nearly to the tip of his nose. Suzie couldn't feel anything but disgust for a man who would trade someone's life for the potential of riches. Jason led him towards the squad car. Once he had Martin secured in the backseat he pulled out his radio and summoned backup to assist with the gathering of evidence. Suzie and Mary remained beside the house, both settled into a quiet state of shock.

"What could possess a man to desire riches so deeply?" Suzie asked softly.

"When you give your life to something you believe it's the most important thing," Mary shook her head. "He lost sight of reality, I'd guess."

Suzie shook her head and drew a deep breath of the salt-laced air. "I just don't understand."

"We're not supposed to," Mary said gently and curled her arm around Suzie's shoulders. "Unfortunately, there are things we will never be able to understand."

"Maybe fortunately," Suzie pointed out as they ascended the steps onto the porch. "Who wants to be able to understand something like that?"

"I'll make us some tea," Mary offered. "You sit on the porch, look out over the water, it will help."

Suzie smiled with gratitude and made her way onto the porch. The opening weekend of Dune House had been hectic, but it was still the most beautiful place to be, according to Suzie. The moment she set eyes on the expanse of blue water before her, she felt the soothing begin. No one could have stopped Doug's murder. It was horrible, and senseless, and Mary was right, she thought, no one should ever be able to understand something like that.

As she looked out over the water she felt her heart expand. She was instinctively searching for the lights of Paul's boat. He had said he would be patient, but Suzie found herself wondering if that was what she really wanted. Why did she pull herself back from such a supportive and romantic relationship?

"Here you are," Mary said as she set down a cup of tea in front of Suzie. Suzie picked up the cup as Mary sat down across from her.

"This has been one eventful day," Mary said softly.

"Yes, it has," Suzie agreed.

"I'm going to meet Jason at the police station," Ben said as he stepped out onto the porch. "Do you two need anything before I go?"

"No," Suzie shook her head.

"Yes," Mary grinned. "We need to know who Jason's girlfriend is."

"Oh Mom," Ben rolled his eyes and then kissed her lightly on the cheek. "I'll see what I can do."

As he jumped down off the porch Mary and Suzie exchanged a long look.

"It's weird to see him all grown up," Suzie giggled. "Does that mean we finally have to be grownups?"

"I don't know about you, but I have no interest

in any of that," Mary smiled warmly.

As they talked Jim and Diana stepped up onto the porch.

"Thanks for telling us about Cheney's," Jim said. "It was delicious."

"When we mentioned we were staying at Dune House, the owner thought you might like this," Diana said as she held out a take-home bag.

Suzie tried not to blush. "Well, I do like pasta," she said with a laugh.

"I noticed the police are no longer here," Jim said. "Is everything settled?"

"Yes," Suzie nodded.

"Good," he smiled and took his wife's hand to lead her inside.

"No need to tell them the whole truth," Mary said softly. "There's nothing like knowing you were sharing a B & B with a killer to ruin a vacation."

"Good point," Suzie nodded. "I'm worn out, I'm going to bed."

"Good night, Suzie," Mary gave her a quick hug before sitting back down at the table. "I'm just going to look at the water for a bit longer."

Suzie studied her for a long moment. She knew that her friend had been through a lot. All of the activity at Dune House had probably made it impossible for her to spend any real time with Ben.

"Are you sure you're okay, Mary?" Suzie asked as she laid a hand lightly on her friend's shoulder.

"Yes, Suzie," she smiled. "Even with all of this chaos, even with all of the uncertainty of opening a B & B, this is still the happiest I've been. I like the adventure, even if I'm just along for the ride."

"Well, something tells me this won't be the last adventure we share," Suzie said with a slightly bitter laugh.

"With the two of us together, you can never

predict," Mary said with a slight smile.

As Suzie walked off to bed she felt herself beginning to relax once more. Dune House was still Dune House, as beautiful and meaningful as it had always been to her.

Chapter Nine

The next morning Suzie awoke with a sense of relief. Something terrible had happened, but at least the killer would be brought to justice. Suzie and Mary said goodbye to the guests who had made it through a dramatic weekend. None looked the worse for wear, other than Martin of course, who was sitting in a jail cell in handcuffs. Diana did still have quite a sunburn but she didn't seem too concerned about it. Jim assured Suzie that they would be back for their free weekend sometime soon. Alice slipped out as quickly as possible. Ever since she had been exposed as a spy she had kept her distance.

"The offer still stands for a free weekend, Alice," Mary said as the woman tried to reach the door without being caught.

"Thanks, but I think next time I want a cold bath, I'll stay local," she smirked at that and sauntered out the door. Suzie knew that Alice might give them bad reviews. She only hoped that they would have enough customers to combat the negative attention. After everyone was gone, Mary and Suzie collapsed on the large, fluffy couch and sighed at the same time.

"That was wild," Suzie said with a shake of her head.

"It was more than wild, it was nuts," Mary clarified.

"I agree," Suzie nodded. "At least we don't have any more guests until next weekend. That should give us some time to get things straightened up, and to recover from this madness."

"That's the truth," Mary agreed and closed her eyes. "Now, I need to take Ben to the airport," she sighed. "I'm going to miss him."

"I know you will," Suzie said. "I hope that he will come again soon."

"I'm sure he will," Mary grinned. "I think he liked being so close to the beach."

"You know, we still haven't found out exactly who Jason is seeing," Suzie pointed out. "One more mystery to solve."

"Oh, I don't think it's too much of a mystery," Mary said with a small smile.

"What do you mean?" Suzie asked.

"I mean I saw the sparkle in his eyes when he looked at Dr. Rose," Mary explained.

"Dr. Rose? The medical examiner?" Suzie asked with surprise "I never thought of that."

"Well, apparently he did," Mary laughed a little. "Ben told me last night that Jason's girlfriend was beautiful, but had a creepy job. I think that confirms it."

"I guess it does," Suzie agreed as she tried to picture the two of them together.

"Do you want me to go with you two to the

airport?" Suzie offered.

"No, I'm sure you'll be watching the water for a certain boat containing a certain captain," she smiled.

"Maybe," Suzie said loftily.

Mary laughed and pushed herself up off the couch. After saying goodbye to Ben, Suzie went about tidying up Dune House.

Suzie was wiping down the kitchen counters with some soft music playing behind her. Her mind had traveled back to her years as an investigative journalist. It had been very exciting to cover stories and to get to know people she never would have met otherwise. However, now she felt as if she was still in the middle of that excitement, but she had Dune House to live in. The walls seemed to breathe secrets as she walked past them.

Dune House had been a source of fascination for locals for many years. Apparently it was also a source of fascination for others. Although the afternoon had been very quiet, she hoped that there would be a visit from Paul soon. She couldn't wait to see his beautiful gray shaded eyes. She still didn't know how to answer his question clearly, but she knew that she had to try. When she heard the front door of Dune House open, a smile began to creep up along her lips.

"Suzie?" Paul's slightly roughened voice called out. Suzie stepped out of the kitchen and met Paul in the dining room.

"Welcome back," she said smoothly as she looked into his eyes. They were filled with concern.

"I heard about what happened, I'm sorry I couldn't get back faster," he frowned as he took Suzie's hands in his and held them gently. "Are you okay?"

"I am now," she replied and kissed him. "I missed you."

"I missed you, too," he murmured as he let go of her hands and wrapped his arms around her waist instead. As he pulled her close to him he looked deeply into her eyes. "I'm sorry if I was pushing too hard."

"You weren't," she smiled fondly.

"I'm still patient," he whispered and kissed her forehead lightly.

"You don't have to be," she replied and kissed him again.

"So, I'm not a liar?" he asked as they both pulled back from the kiss, a smile playing on his lips.

"No, you're not a liar," she replied with confidence in her voice. As they kissed again, Suzie felt the last of her resolve fading. Just as Paul coming home to dry land was his safe harbor, being wrapped up in his arms, had become hers.

The End

More Cozy Mysteries by Cindy Bell

Dune House Cozy Mystery Series

Seaside Secrets

Boats and Bad Guys

Treasured History

Hidden Hideaways

Heavenly Highland Inn Cozy Mystery Series

Murdering the Roses

Dead in the Daisies

Killing the Carnations

Drowning the Daffodils

Suffocating the Sunflowers

Books, Bullets and Blooms

A Deadly serious Gardening Contest

Wendy the Wedding Planner Cozy Mystery Series

Matrimony, Money and Murder

Chefs, Ceremonies and Crimes

Bekki the Beautician Cozy Mystery Series

Hairspray and Homicide

A Dyed Blonde and a Dead Body

Mascara and Murder

Pageant and Poison

Conditioner and a Corpse

Mistletoe, Makeup and Murder

Hairpin, Hair Dryer and Homicide

Blush, a Bride and a Body

Shampoo and a Stiff

Cosmetics, a Cruise and a Killer

Lipstick, a Long Iron and Lifeless

Camping, Concealer and Criminals